Take no prisoners

Glass and blood, briefly glowing in the spotlight, exploded in a circular cloud. Another frantic scream rose above the engine's whine as the jeep swerved left, hurling the gunner into the cactus spears. Carl Lyons fired again as a second jeep swung in from behind the clustered creosote bushes. Then his eyes locked on to the eyes of the bulky gunner from the first jeep.

The soldier was young, no more than twenty; and although the eyes were alive with fury, the innocence was unmistakable. I know that kid, Lyons thought vaguely. I faced him on the mats, showed him how to reverse a choke-hold and how to sweep a leg. He also recalled having showed the kid how to load and fire a Browning P-53 on a roll, which was exactly what the kid was doing now....

"Able Team will go anywhere, do anything, in order to complete their mission."
—*West Coast Review of Books*

Mack Bolan's

ABLE TEAM®

#1 Tower of Terror

#2 The Hostaged Island

#3 Texas Showdown

#4 Amazon Slaughter

#5 Cairo Countdown

#6 Warlord of Azatlan

#7 Justice by Fire

#8 Army of Devils

#9 Kill School

#10 Royal Flush

#11 Five Rings of Fire

#12 Deathbites

#13 Scorched Earth

#14 Into the Maze

#15 They Came to Kill

#16 Rain of Doom

#17 Fire and Maneuver

#18 Tech War

#19 Ironman

#20 Shot to Hell

#21 Death Strike

#22 The World War III Game

#23 Fall Back and Kill

#24 Blood Gambit

#25 Hard Kill

#26 The Iron God

#27 Cajun Angel

#28 Miami Crush

#29 Death Ride

#30 Hit and Run

#31 Ghost Train

#32 Firecross

#33 Cowboy's Revenge

#34 Clear Shot

#35 Strike Force

#36 Final Run

#37 Red Menace

#38 Cold Steel

#39 Death Code

#40 Blood Mark

#41 White Fire

#42 Dead Zone

#43 Kill Orbit

#44 Night Heat

#45 Lethal Trade

#46 Counterblow

#47 Shadow Warriors

ABLE TEAM.

Shadow Warriors

Dick Stivers

A GOLD EAGLE BOOK FROM
W☉RLDWIDE.

TORONTO • NEW YORK • LONDON • PARIS
AMSTERDAM • STOCKHOLM • HAMBURG
ATHENS • MILAN • TOKYO • SYDNEY

First edition April 1990

ISBN 0-373-61247-8

Special thanks and acknowledgment to
Ken Rose for his contribution to this work.

1

The report submitted by Internal Security stated that Staff Sergeant Harold Gibb left the Game Room at exactly 1900 hours. From there he proceeded to Central Files, where he withdrew at least two volumes of analysis documenting the March and April "Capital Defense" games. Challenged by Security Officer Andrew Harper, Gibb explained that he was acting under orders from Company Commander W. T. Stack, USA. When Security Officer Harper insisted that the order be verified, Gibb picked up a staple gun and struck the man repeatedly about the face and head. The beating resulted in massive contusions, a fractured jaw and loss of consciousness. Gibb then proceeded along D corridor until he reached the gates of the Domestic Insurrection Response compound—the Wolf's Tooth Complex. Thereafter his movements were described as a "headlong flight into the New Mexico night."

There was a storm the night that Harold Gibb fled the Wolf's Tooth compound, and it was to prove a factor in the subsequent hunt. Prior to his posting with the Domestic Insurrection Response group, Gibb had served three tours in Vietnam with the Special Forces. Thus once he reached the high chaparral, not even the wind and slanting rain could stop him. He'd worked well under those conditions.

Gibb was a slender man, with mousy-brown hair and a face that belied his forty-two years. Although generally regarded as presentable, by the time he reached the mesa road, he was an alarming sight. Not only was his uniform drenched and torn, he had also suffered a six-inch cut above his left eye while crawling through the sagebrush. It was not until ten o'clock that he finally managed to convince a passing motorist that he was not an escaped convict.

The driver turned out to be a nineteen-year-old New Mexico University student by the name of Molly Meekin. She was a pretty girl, in a plain sort of way. Slender and boyish with a shaggy mane of blond hair, she was everyone's picture of the local Corn Queen from Iowa. In fact, however, she was originally from Palm Beach; and the only reason she stopped her battered Honda to pick up Harold Gibb was that she genuinely thought he was hurt.

"You all right?" Molly asked after she had eased her Honda onto the gravel shoulder and had cautiously rolled down the window.

"I don't know," Gibb replied, desperately trying to appear sane and innocent. "I had an accident. If you could take me to a telephone."

She hesitated, left foot still on the clutch, gears still engaged . . . briefly recalling the modus operandi of recently convicted serial killers.

"Okay." She nodded. "Get in."

In all the mesa road wound approximately seven miles from the high desert plateau where the Wolf's Tooth compound lay to the main highway below. It was seven tortuous miles along the sandstone buttes made all the more dangerous by the storm. Although Gibb would have preferred to remain silent through the course of this journey, he knew that he couldn't entirely avoid conversation if he hoped to reassure this nervous girl.

"I guess I kind of lost it," he said as they eased back onto the road. "One moment I was cruising into a turn, next moment I was crawling through the windshield."

"Were you driving alone?" the girl asked.

"Yeah, thank God."

"Well, that's a pretty nasty cut you've got there. Maybe I should take you to a hospital."

Gibb gingerly touched the gash on his forehead. "Nah, it's all right. I think just a phone will do me fine."

He felt her eyeing his reflection in the windshield.

"You're not from that secret base on the mesa, are you?" she finally asked.

Gibb shifted his gaze from the rainwashed road to the girl's pretty profile. "Huh?"

"Your uniform."

He grinned. "Oh yeah, my uniform."

"So are you?"

"Am I what?"

"From that secret base on the Wolf's Tooth Mesa?"

He grinned again. "What secret base?"

"Come on, it's not like it hasn't been in the news. The place where they hold all those war maneuvers and stuff."

Gibb returned his eyes to the blackened desert road and settled a little deeper into the seat. Then finally deciding that it no longer made any difference, he breathed, "Yeah, I'm from that base in the hills."

"So what's the real story?" she asked.

Gibb looked at her. "What do you mean?"

"I mean, what's really going on up there? You guys planning for World War III, or are you just trying to keep the peace?"

Gibb allowed himself a slight smile as he recalled his initial excitement and enthusiasm when first asked to join America's most elite military planning and response group.

"I guess you could say that we're kind of playing it down the middle," he answered.

They had approximately six more miles of blackened highway ahead of them. Although Gibb had driven this stretch at least a hundred times, it could not have looked more alien—a long, forbidding strip of pavement between the black humps of Indian mounds and volcanically fused rock. Dark shadows, sweeping across the distant chaparral suggested they were being watched. Peals of thunder suggested cannon fire.

"I mean it's not like I got anything against the military," she said. "It's just that...well, sometimes you can't help but feel a little paranoid."

Another dark shadow crossed the road, possibly a deer or a coyote. Another burst of thunder rolled in like mortar fire from the north.

"Paranoid about what?" he asked.

She shrugged. "You know, military takeover. Police state. That sort of thing."

Gibb shut his eyes and took a deep breath. "Yeah, well I wouldn't worry about it." He sighed. "After all, this ain't no banana republic. This is the USA."

They drove in silence for another five miles: Gibb shutting his eyes again and fixing his attention on the lonely clack of windshield wipers; Molly whispering snatches of an old Buffalo Springfield song that urged its listeners "to beware."

She suddenly broke off and pointed to a row of faint lights in the distance. "How about I stop over there?" she asked.

Gibb opened his eyes and peered through the rain-streaked glass to the darkened outline of a lonely desert service station and what may have been a diner. Although the place appeared closed, there was definitely a telephone booth. And more importantly, there was no one in sight.

"Yeah." He sighed. "I think that'll be fine."

Molly turned off the highway and proceeded slowly until she reached the entrance to the gas station. In addition to a rank of pumps and a service bay, there was also a four-booth diner called Last Chance Café.

"Well, I really want to thank you for the lift," Gibb said as the Honda eased to a stop.

The girl gave him a sideways glance. "Don't you want me to wait?"

Gibb shook his head with an easy grin. "No, that's okay. I'll just call the auto club. They're usually pretty fast."

"Don't be silly. You could be stuck out here for another two hours."

"Yeah, well I don't want to impose anymore than I already have."

She cocked her head with an equally easy smile. "Look, it's not an imposition. Besides, if you guys really are planning to take over the country, I'm going to need a friend on the inside."

He glanced out to the empty highway, then back to her warm smile. "Okay, I'll make that call and be right back."

Although Gibb must have mentally rehearsed this call at least a hundred times through the weeks preceding his flight from the compound, he suddenly felt himself losing control as he stepped into the phone booth. He couldn't seem to locate his change, then couldn't seem to slip the damn quarters into the slot. His hands were shaking so badly, he could hardly hit the buttons with his finger.

He counted six rings, six endless rings, before a woman finally came on the line with a cool and practised greeting, "Senator Harwood's residence."

Gibb shut his eyes and took another long breath to calm his nerves.

"Senator John Harwood's residence?" he asked.

"That's correct," the woman replied.

"My name is Harold. Harold Gibb."

"Yes, Mr. Gibb. How can I help you?"

"I've got to speak to the senator."

A slight pause, maybe even a whisper.

"I'm sorry, Mr. Gibb. The senator is not available right now. If you'd like to call his office on Monday, I'm sure—"

"Look, you don't understand. I've got to speak to him *now*."

Another pause, this one slightly longer.

"I'm terribly sorry, but that's quite impossible. Now, if you'd care to leave a message I'll be sure he gets it the moment he comes in."

Gibb pressed his face against the cool glass, staring out through sheets of rain to what looked like approaching headlights off in the distance.

"Mr. Gibb?"

"Look, this isn't just a social call. This is an emergency. A matter of life or death."

The lights seemed to slow, possibly in order for the vehicle to exit the highway.

"Well, all I can suggest, sir, is that you leave a message."

"A message?"

The approaching headlights swept the pavement in a long and closing arc.

"Yes, if you care to leave the senator a message, I'll be happy to—"

"Okay, tell him...tell him that it's about the Wolf's Tooth compound."

"The Wolf's Tooth?"

"That's right, the Wolf's Tooth. Tell him it's about the games being played at the Wolf's Tooth. The counterinsurrection games."

"Counterinsurrection? Now, is that one word or two?"

The headlights burst in his eyes like a thousand popping flashbulbs and the echo of a roaring engine filled his ears.

"Look, just tell him that the counterinsurrection game is not a game!" he shouted. "Do you understand? It's *not a game!*"

Then, although the woman may have muttered some sort of startled reply, it was lost in the scream and rattling burst of autofire.

MOLLY MEEKIN ACTUALLY HEARD Gibb scream twice—first as the black sedan swerved into a turn and a hunched figure beside the driver extended a rifle through the window, then again as the phone booth exploded in glass and blood.

There was a third scream as Gibb's eyes went wide with shock and pain, but she supposed that it was her own. She screamed a second time as the hunched figure leaped from the sedan and she caught a glimpse of his eyes in the rearview mirror...eyes locking onto her eyes.

She turned the ignition, whispering, "Oh, God, please. *Please!*" She heard the engine straining to catch, finally heard it roar to life before she jammed the gearshift into first. She heard herself whispering again, "Oh, God, please," as she popped the clutch and felt the Honda lurching forward. Then she heard herself scream yet again as those eyes in the rearview mirror narrowed to slits and four quick bursts of flame flashed from the muzzle of his rifle.

The Honda spun hard to the left, the engine straining with a sickening whine of splintering metal before finally grinding to a halt. Someone shouted. "Hold your fire! You read me, Corporal? Hold your fire!" She caught a glimpse of a second face peering through the shattered windshield—a clean-shaven young man with a military crew cut and the bluest eyes she'd ever seen. She felt the rush of icy air as the door flew open, and cold hands clamped around her wrists....

Molly screamed again as they dragged her from behind the wheel and pinned her shoulders to the wet pavement.

And Blue Eyes smiled, "Don't worry, honey. United States Army. We're on your side, okay?"

2

Senator Harwood had never particularly enjoyed his luncheons with the generals at the Pentagon. Part of his distaste for these affairs stemmed from the fact that, as the most outspoken liberal on the Armed Services Committee, he knew he was not the military's favorite legislator. But there was also something else—Harwood had a deep and truly profound distrust of America's killing machine.

A lean and ruggedly handsome man, Harwood was serving his fifth year as senior senator for the great state of Maine. On the whole, they had been thankless years. For his opposition to the Stealth Bomber and the MX Missile System, he had been called everything from a spineless pinko to a Commie dupe—and that was just what they called him to his face. He had further caught a fair amount of flak for his environmental stance, which favored complete elimination of fossil fuel by 1999 and a severe review of the nation's nuclear power operations. And to make matters worse, he was known to be an accomplished poet who wore tattersall shirts, corduroy jackets, bow ties and oxfords.

It was exactly twelve o'clock when Harwood pulled his slightly battered Chevrolet into the parking lot of the Pentagon. The sky was cloudless and a deep blue. The air was crisp with a breeze off the river. Although only three days had passed since the senator's last haircut, he still had that vaguely disheveled look the generals hated. It was a look that said: bleeding heart liberal with a razor wit.

Regardless of what the generals may have privately felt about Harwood, they never forgot that he was still a member of the committee that approved the Pentagon's budget. He was never treated with anything less than absolute respect whenever he entered the warrior's palace. Upon moving past the electronic checkpoint, for example, he was always greeted civilly. And he was always treated to lunch of either lobster or duck in one of the exclusive fifth-floor conference rooms.

On this particular Wednesday afternoon, Harwood's host was none other than Joint Chiefs of Staff Chairman, General Raymond R. Doyle, otherwise known as Rambling Ray Doyle. Also present was JCS General Arthur Matoon Clancy and Joint Staff Planning Director, General Robert "the Shark" Maloy. Together with the JCS Admiral William "the Kid" Jones, these men were said to be a power unto themselves—the most effective, and yet secretive military foursome the nation had ever seen. The President, however, loved them and not even Harwood could fault their performance during the second Iranian hostage crisis.

Typically the meeting began with what Harwood would have described as an icy cordiality. Although the senator had originally requested to meet only with Maloy, he was told that the big guns had decided to join them on more or less the spur of the moment.

"Because it's always a rare pleasure to see you, Senator," said the lean and silver-haired Doyle in his soft-spoken Southern drawl.

"My sentiments exactly," added the squarely built General Clancy with a slight Tennessean twang.

The room they sat in could not have been more reflective of Pentagon mentality: stark, windowless and predominantly brown. Apart from the bullet-shredded Old Glory and the regulation photograph of the President, the walls were bare. There was, however, a plastic model of the Stealth Bomber and another model of a sixty-billion-dollar weapon that Harwood vehemently opposed.

"Well now, Senator, why don't you tell us exactly how we can be of service to you?" Maloy began. A sleek and meticulously groomed young man in his early forties, Maloy was said to be the Army's brightest hope for a Communist-free future. He was also regarded as the only Pentagon heavy with real political flair and consequently there was always talk of running him for one of the congressional seats.

"I guess you might call this a sort of fact-finding mission," Harwood replied with a razor thin smile. "I guess you might call it a sort of unofficial fact-finding mission."

"Well, unofficial doesn't bother us," Maloy said with an equally thin smile. "In fact, unofficial suits us just fine."

Neither Doyle nor Clancy, however, seemed even remotely amused.

"To put it bluntly," Harwood continued, "it concerns one of your western installations."

"One of our western installations, Senator?" Maloy asked.

Harwood withdrew a crumpled piece of stationery from his coat pocket. "Something called the Wolf's Tooth Complex, which is apparently located somewhere on the mesa."

Maloy ran a thoughtful hand through his close cropped hair, while the other generals exchanged quick glances.

"The mesa, huh?" Maloy said. "If memory serves me correctly that would be in—"

"New Mexico," Doyle said with a hard grin. "Used to know the place real well. Not too far from Albuquerque, kind of between Kirtland and Sandia on the cusp of one of those Indian reservations. Cold as hell this time of year, but not too bad in the spring. Nice hunting, too, if you got the stomach for that kind thing."

"So what do they do out there?" Harwood asked.

"Do?" Doyle smiled.

"At the Wolf's Tooth."

Doyle smiled again, exchanging another glance with the stocky General Clancy. "Why, they don't do much of anything . . . that I'm at liberty to talk about, Senator."

Two trim enlisted men appeared, with trays of coffee and canapés. Also on the menu was iced shrimp and oysters on the half-shell.

"I think what the general here is trying to tell you," Clancy said, "is that although the Wolf's Tooth compound is a relatively insignificant establishment, what goes on there happens to be classified right now."

"Classified by whom?"

"Well, the chairman of your committee for starters."

"Then maybe I'll just have to go to the chairman and ask him to declassify it."

There was another brief exchange of glances and then Doyle apparently nodded to Maloy.

"I'll tell you what," Maloy said at last. "How about you fill us in on why you're so interested in this business and we'll do our best to satisfy your curiosity?"

Harwood took a deep breath, exhaling slowly through his teeth. "All right, then let me put it like this. I received a telephone call from a young man stationed out there, a young man who was very concerned about recent happenings at the site."

"May we know what specifically concerned this man?" Doyle asked.

"Let's just say that it involved possible violations of civil rights."

"And these concerns were definitely lodged by one of our personnel?" Maloy asked.

"That's correct."

"One of our personnel stationed at the Wolf's Tooth?" Clancy repeated.

"Correct."

"Well, in that case we don't really know what to tell you, Senator," Doyle said with a broad grin.

"Except maybe to offer our apologies on behalf of all men in uniform," Maloy added.

Harwood lowered his left hand below the table, and clenched it into a fist. His expression, however, remained calm while the fingers of his right hand continued to idly pick at a neatly skewered shrimp.

"I assure you, gentlemen, that the boy who called me wasn't just another sniveler looking for a transfer. He was a young man who had seen something out there that made him concerned . . . real concerned about the way your Army is being run."

"But unless you can offer us specific charges of abuse or neglect," Clancy returned, "I hardly see what we can do."

"Apart from a routine investigation, of course," Doyle added.

"Which, with your permission sir, I'll initiate immediately," Maloy said.

Once again Harwood clenched a hidden fist in order to control his simmering rage. Then, finally taking a slow and deep breath, he finally tossed his napkin down and rose from the table.

"Gentlemen," he said addressing all three, "I'm not going to play games with you anymore. A few nights ago a member of my staff received a phone call from a clearly agitated soldier. Now, ordinarily I might not take that kind of call too seriously. But for some reason I got a feeling about this one, possibly due to the fact that the man has subsequently disappeared from the face of the earth. So if it's all the same to you, I think I'm going to conduct my own investigation. Good day."

Although Maloy attempted to rise from the table to reply with a few choice words of his own, General Doyle kept him in his place with his iron grip.

FOR SEVERAL HOURS following his luncheon with the generals, Harwood simply drifted. He returned to the Hill for pointless meetings with lobbyists from the defense industry. He wasted forty minutes with a distinguished representative from Colorado. He leafed through stacks of pending bills and their meaningless amendments.

Then at exactly half past four in the afternoon, after slipping out to use a public phone, he called Lyle Severson at the Central Intelligence Agency in Langley, Virginia.

ALTHOUGH TECHNICALLY a member of the enemy camp, Lyle Severson was one of the few men in government that Harwood could genuinely count as a friend. Their friendship extended back to the years they'd shared a room at Harvard, a Jaguar with a faulty ignition, a tabby named Harcourt and, on one occasion, a girlfriend. Of course, there had been times when they hadn't exactly seen eye-to-eye on certain issues of state, times when they had all but come to blows over this or that foreign initiative. But when the chips were down, they had always found that they could count on one another for a discreet and subtle helping hand.

Physically, Severson was a tall and angular man, with long wisps of snow white hair and pale gray eyes. After catching a piece of shrapnel in some obscure and secret Asian war, he tended to favor his left leg—particularly in damp weather. He occasionally suffered from nightmares, owing to a seven-month stint in an East German prison and it was rumored that he still carried a 9 mm slug in his hip— a farewell present from a Soviet colonel.

Yet for all the knocks that Severson had suffered through his years of service to the country, he was still a gentle soul. Like Harwood, he considered himself a poet and had actually published three slim volumes under the name of D. Michael Sherman. He was also rumored to have led a secret life with a twenty-eight-year-old ballerina from New York.

It was seven o'clock in the evening when Severson and Harwood finally managed to rendezvous. At Severson's suggestion, they met in a half-forgotten Travel Lodge off a lonely stretch of highway along the Piedmont. The room, secured under the name of Henderson, was plain and cold, with frayed curtains and a threadbare rug. There was a hot plate and a junked refrigerator, a radio but no television.

It began on what struck the senator as a positively chilling note. The radio was switched on, the telephone unplugged and buried beneath a pillow. Then drawing the curtains closed, Severson removed a nonlinear junction detector for a quick sweep of the walls.

"Is all this really necessary?" Harwood asked.

Severson shrugged while stooping to examine the underside of the coffee table. "That depends upon what you mean by necessary."

"Come on, Lyle, you know what I mean."

Apparently satisfied with this cursory search, Severson retired to the sagging sofa with a flask of Johnny Walker.

"Let me put it like this," he said. "You wouldn't smoke cigarettes when you're pumping gas, would you?"

In addition to the Scotch, Severson had also brought two bottles of a local mineral water. There was no ice, however, and the water tasted faintly of copper.

"All right then," Harwood said after accepting a none too clean glass, "what's the bottom line?"

Severson shook his head with a dull sigh and took a first cautious sip. "Hard to say really. But I can tell you this, you're definitely tugging on a live wire."

"In what sense?"

"In the sense that this so-called Wolf's Tooth Complex is one very closely guarded secret."

Harwood also took a cautious sip. "Fine, but what are the parameters? Who the hell is Harold Gibb?"

"Oh, he exists all right."

"And?"

"And nothing." Severson smiled. "He was transferred out to the Wolf's Tooth from Special Forces about twenty months ago. He was listed as a staff analyst with a double A security rating. Beyond that, I can't find out a thing."

"So what the hell did he mean when he told my secretary that it wasn't a game? Hmm? What the hell does it all mean?"

Severson also took a sip of Scotch, then moved to the window and slowly inched back the curtains. In a perfect world he would have brought at least two members from the covert action staff to watch his back. As it was, however, he had to rely on instinct and his remarkably keen vision.

"What do you know about the D.I.R. group?" he asked at last.

"The what?"

"Domestic Insurrection Response."

"Never heard of it."

"Brainchild of a Hudson River think tank called the Hastings Strategic Advisory Institute."

"You mean Dick Turk's group."

"Among others."

"So what's the story?"

"A two-hundred-plus-page report entitled, 'An Examination of Liabilities Concerning Domestic Insurrection, Mass Terrorism and Civil Unrest'."

"With footnotes?"

"Dozens of them. But it's not a joke, Johnny. It's a very seriously written document."

"Regarding?"

"Life in the 1990s. Life in a nation where the gap between the rich and the poor has become a mile wide festering wound, breeding all sorts of unhealthy strains."

"And the solution is the Domestic Insurrection Response?"

"Exactly."

Severson returned from the window and slumped back down on the sofa. Up until now the radio had been playing selections from Vivaldi's *Magnificat*, but it suddenly switched to J. S. Bach. There were also cries of crows outside and the occasional rattle of passing trucks loaded with freshly cut Christmas trees.

"Now, understand I'm not saying it's right or wrong," Severson continued against the cold notes of a harpsichord. "I'm just giving you the facts."

"Sure." Harwood sighed as an even colder sense of dread began to spread from the pit of his stomach. "You're just giving me the facts."

"By 1990, this nation will very possibly be closer to a state of open rebellion than at any time in our history. And we're not just talking about riots in the ghetto. We're talking about a spontaneous and massive urban conflagration, ultimately involving hundreds of thousands of individuals across dozens of cities nationwide.''

"And what do they say will be the spark?''

"Could be anything. Assassination of a popular leader. Nationally advertised case of police brutality. Sudden economic decline. Anything.''

Harwood took another sip of Scotch and shook his head. "Sounds unlikely to me,'' he said.

"Not if you factor in covert foreign support in the way of sophisticated arms and teams to train the people to use those arms. Anyway, I'm not trying to convince you, John, I'm just telling you what the scenario is. I'm just saying that there are people out there in this government who sincerely believe that a massive civilian insurrection is not only possible but probable sometime in the next ten years.''

"And I suppose the solution to this so-called probable insurrection is the Wolf's Tooth?''

Severson nodded. "Far as I can tell from the cable traffic, yes. The Wolf's Tooth was set up about fifteen months ago as a short notice response unit designed to move at the first sign of domestic rebellion.''

"Okay, but who are they? Where did they come from?''

Severson shook his head, rising from the sofa to pace the room as the radio began to play selections from Tchaikovsky's *Swan Lake*.

"I can give you a theory,'' he said at last, "an educated guess based on fragments I've managed to pick up here and there from internal memos.''

"Fine,'' Harwood breathed. "So give me a theory.''

"All right, let's say you're General Rambling Ray Doyle or one of the other Pentagon heavies and you've just been given an order to establish a unit like the D.I.R., a unit that might one day be asked to quash a domestic rebellion of frustrated American citizens. Now, where are you going to form that group? Where are you going to find fifteen hundred soldiers who can face a crowd of their fellow Americans and pull the trigger without a second thought?''

"I'd get them from the Special Forces," Harwood said softly.

"Exactly," Severson replied. "You'd get them from the Special Forces. You'd pick them up from the SEALs and the Black Berets. You'd sheep-deep them from every hard-line unit this side of China, because ultimately that's what you want: the professionals, borderline psychos, the guys who don't give a shit that the enemy happens to be the kid next door just so long as they're getting paid.''

Now it was Harwood's turn to rise from the sofa and thoughtfully pace the room. "So what the hell are they doing out there?" he finally asked.

"Games," Severson replied. "They're waiting for the insurrection and playing games."

"What do you mean by playing games?"

"Exactly that—games. Someone gives them a scenario: a rebel strike force, backed by Cuban mercs, has just taken over downtown Detroit. They're holding fifty hostages, including the mayor, and they're armed to the teeth with antipersonnel weapons. Now, what are you going to do about it?"

"And these games are conducted from computer models?"

"For the most part, yeah."

"Then unless they've got an entirely closed system, there's got to be a way to tap in and read the score."

Severson took another sip of Scotch and then bit his lower lip. "Before you start playing James Bond, old buddy, I think there's something you'd better understand. That Wolf's Tooth unit may be playing games, but by the same token they're also playing for keeps."

Harwood turned from staring out at the landscape. "What's that supposed to mean?"

"It means that I think you'd better watch your step. It means that until we know just how far this thing goes, I think you'd better take it real slow."

"You mean to say that—"

"I'm not sure what I'm saying, except that we may be up against some very serious weight here and I'd hate to see it land on your head."

"So what are you suggesting? That we do nothing? That we walk away and forget the whole thing?"

Severson shook his head. "I'm suggesting that we don't do anything stupid. That we don't go asking the wrong questions from the wrong people. That we don't use private telephones when we know very well that these people probably have the capability of tapping every line on the Hill. That you don't do anything that deviates from your normal routine. I'm also suggesting that you watch your back twenty-four hours a day, and I mean that very literally."

Harwood shifted his gaze back to the window and the narrow view through parted curtains of the highway stretching between the pines.

"Don't you think you're overreacting a little?" he said at last.

Severson took another weary breath and another nervous mouthful of Scotch. "I hope so, old buddy. I hope so."

DUSK WAS FALLING when Harwood left the motor lodge, a chilled dusk that would soon leave the gutters encrusted with ice and the broad lawns layered with frost. Although he had previously agreed to meet the junior senator from Colorado at the Arlington Athletic Club for their weekly round of racquetball, he finally decided that he simply didn't have the strength. Yet after placing a call on his cellular phone to cancel the appointment, he suddenly remembered Severson's warning: *Don't do anything that deviates from your normal routine.*

It was dark by the time Harwood reached the Washington Memorial Highway and the last long stretch of road to his home. According to local legend, there were ghosts in the hills beyond the causeway—restless ghosts of Indians to whom this land had once belonged, angry ghosts of thieves who had been hanged more than two hundred years ago. Even the sad ghosts of Confederate soldiers were reported to roam the rolling hills surrounding the capital.

In the end, however, it was the ghost of a flat brown Pontiac that left Harwood chilled to the bone.

He first caught sight of the car as he neared Bear's Neck Run. Although there were any number of headlights in his rearview mirror, something about that Pontiac immediately concerned him...something about the fact that it continued to maintain a constant distance regardless of whether he sped up or slowed down. He also didn't like the look of the driver and the short-haired passenger who appeared to be scanning the road ahead with some sort of night-vision system. When he finally eased off the highway onto Bear's Neck Road, there was no denying that he was being followed.

Between the Memorial Highway exit and Harwood's mock Tudor hillside cottage, lay seven twisted miles of dark and narrow road. Over the years there had been dozens of accidents along the treacherous curves and more than one luckless motorist had plunged through the railing and into the deep ponds below. But of all the hazardous twists and turns, nothing seemed quite so disturbing to Harwood as the last three miles above the Black Swan Creek.

The creek lay approximately sixty feet below the road's narrow shoulder, sixty feet to a dark and shadowy marsh.

Every three or four years, after yet another motorist plunged to his death, one heard talk from local civic groups of erecting an impact-proof guardrail. But like so much else in and around Washington, the talk amounted to nothing.

Harwood slowed as he neared the creek, briefly forgetting the trailing Pontiac, thinking only of black ice and oil slicks, blowouts and brake failures. Then lifting his eyes to the rearview mirror, he saw that the car was virtually on top of him. He pressed the accelerator halfway to the floor and felt the tires shudder over the potholes. He eased his Chevy away from the shoulder, caught another glimpse of the Pontiac and swerved to avoid an impact. They're trying to run me off the road, he thought dully. He swerved again as the Pontiac drew parallel with his Chevy.

The first impact was like a sudden slap from a giant's hand, a firm and jolting hit to his right fender. He felt the wheel shudder, heard the tires squealing as steel folded under steel. The second impact left him breathless, desperately straining to keep the Chevy off the gravel shoulder. Then came a third and fourth slap as the whole of the Pontiac's body swerved in with deadly precision.

There was blood in Harwood's mouth and he vaguely realized that he must have bitten his lip. There was glass on the dashboard and he supposed that the impact must have shattered the window. He chanced a quick glance to his right and caught another glimpse of the face behind the Pontiac's wheel. It was a young and determined face, the sort of face that one saw gracing Marine Corps recruitment ads. But as the man slowly turned to meet his gaze, Harwood noticed something else: a complete absence of any recognizable emotion.

There was the sickening crunch as the Pontiac's fender slammed into the Chevy's door. Harwood felt the wheel briefly turn to rubber in his hands, the rear tires briefly slipping on the shoulder and the clatter of gravel in the wheel wells. He eased up on the accelerator until he felt pavement beneath his tires. Then turning his head an inch to the right and catching another quick glimpse at that clean-shaven face, he knew what was happening. He knew that they were actually trying to kill him!

He felt the impact of yet another sideswipe, then heard the screech of rubber on gravel. Although it fleetingly crossed his mind that he ought to jam the wheel left, his natural response was to the right. . . .

That movement left him hanging, literally hanging for a full three seconds as the Chevy hurtled through the railing and into the blackness below. Then it vaguely crossed his mind that he really ought to brace his head against his arms, shut his eyes and close his mouth. But in the end he rode it down, wide-eyed and with a scream that seemed to echo in his ears long after he lapsed into unconsciousness.

How long Harwood lay among the wreckage of his Chevy, he would never really know for certain. He was only conscious of the little things: the echo of crickets in the tall reeds, the call of bullfrogs from across the water, a dull pain in ribs and legs and the slowly oozing mud that softened the impact and probably saved his life. Finally, after what must have been at least an hour, he was also conscious of voices . . . the remarkably calm and collected voices of men who were used to dragging people off Black Rock Creek.

3

Although generally regarded as one of the last great liberal Democrats, Senator Harwood could be as aggressive as any Conservative Republican when circumstances called for it. When neo-Nazis raised their ugly heads in North Dakota, for example, Harwood had been the first to call for a massive armed response. Likewise, he had been one of the first to advocate firing upon Japanese fishing vessels caught slaughtering dolphins in United States waters, and even recommended a rescue operation to secure the release of two U.S. students illegally jailed in Spain.

But never had Harwood ever dreamed of enlisting the help of the kind of men that Severson brought him on the ninth day of his convalescence.

It was a Friday, a cold but clear Friday morning, with the first real sense of Christmas in the air. Although Harwood had been released from Georgetown Medical two days earlier, he was still largely immobile. In addition to four shattered ribs, he had suffered a punctured lung and a severe concussion. He was also frightened...which was ultimately the reason why Severson had brought him the three men.

Harwood was seated on the glass-enclosed patio when Severson and the three men arrived. From the patio one had a long view of the road below Harwood's house and the winding flagstone path leading to its entrance. Therefore, although Harwood was not in a position to answer the door, he actually saw the men well in advance of their arrival.

At first glance the three men looked like cops or private investigators. The tallest one wore a checked sport coat, probably purchased off the rack. Probably purchased at a discount house. Although obviously muscular, he seemed to possess the flexible strength of a swimmer or even a dancer. The blond hair and relatively youthful features seemed at odds with the eyes. The shortest one wore a blue windbreaker and black pants. Apparently of Hispanic origin, he was dark and wiry with what must be an extremely agile strength. The third man, also in black slacks and a windbreaker, was built like a prize fighter. Despite their differences in appearance, Harwood immediately noticed that all three had one thing in common: a predatory grace that seemed evident in every movement, every glance, every flick of the eye.

"Gentlemen, I'd like you to meet Senator John Harwood," Severson said as he led his three guests to the patio. Then turning to Harwood with a sly smile, "Senator, I'd like you to meet my colleagues. This is Carl Lyons," he said, indicating the tall, blond one. "This is Gadgets Schwarz and Rosario Blancanales." Then came the handshakes, the brief exchange of amenities, and finally a call to the housekeeper for a round of cool drinks.

The conversation once more started on a vaguely menacing note. Having seated himself between Lyons and Blancanales, Severson turned to Harwood and began absently toying with his wedding band—a gesture that he often employed when discussing such delicate subjects as the placing of agents or assassination teams.

"To put it bluntly, John, these gentlemen represent a slightly more direct solution than what we had previously discussed," he began. "But given what happened to you on the road the other night, I feel the time has come to think in terms of direct solutions.''

Harwood glanced into Lyons's eyes, then at his hands, then at the telltale bulge beneath the checked sport coat. The one named Blancanales was also undoubtedly carrying a weapon beneath his jacket, while the one called Schwarz may have been wearing an ankle holster.

''And by a direct solution,'' Harwood finally said, ''you mean exactly what?''

Severson shrugged while continuing to rotate that ring on his finger. ''How about we call it an aggressive investigation?''

''How aggressive?''

''Very.''

Harwood shifted in his easy chair to relieve the pressure on his ribs. There was nothing, however, he could do about the mounting pressure in the air.

''You know, I don't have the authority to okay an operation like this,'' he said at last.

Severson shrugged again. ''That's okay. These gentlemen carry their own authority.''

''Under what kind of legal mandate?''

Severson shifted his gaze to Lyons and grinned. ''Let's just call it the law of the jungle, shall we?''

The drinks arrived, along with a message that the senior senator from Kansas was on the phone. Without even bothering to consider the matter, Harwood ordered his housekeeper to take a message.

''At this point it's really just a question of basic survival,'' Severson said.

''You mean 'survival of the fittest'?'' Harwood replied with a thin smile.

Severson nodded, also smiling. ''Something like that, yes. Because what's the bottom line here? The bottom line is that two probable military personnel tried to kill you last week. Now they may have been just a couple of punks having fun, but I don't think so. I think they were acting on orders from above, high above.''

"And so you're suggesting that we enlist these gentlemen here to—''

"What I'm suggesting, John, is this: you're a political animal. You know your way around the conference table and you can make some pretty mean telephone calls. But what you're facing now is something that you've probably never seen before—the worst kind of executive action. Now, I don't know exactly who's behind it, how deep it goes or where it's headed; but I do know that you're not going to resolve it with a power lunch.''

Harwood shifted in his chair again to relieve the pressure on his aching leg. Although it wasn't warm, he also noticed that he had begun to perspire.

"How do you suggest we start?'' he asked.

Severson turned to Lyons, and nodded.

"Well, to begin with,'' Lyons said, "I think we should probably take a look at that Wolf's Tooth compound . . . a close look.''

"How do you expect to manage that?''

"It so happens that these gentlemen are experts on the subject of counterterrorism,'' Severson replied. "Now, it doesn't seem too unreasonable to me that they should be invited in as—how shall I put it? Special guest instructors?''

"And exactly how do you plan to arrange that kind of invitation?'' Harwood asked.

"Let us worry about that,'' Blancanales said.

"The point being,'' Severson added, "that if we can get these men on the inside, we can begin to deal with this thing on an effective level.''

"And by effective, you mean?"

"I mean strategically."

"With force?"

"If necessary."

"And what if there's counterforce?"

Severson smiled again, exchanging a quick glance with Schwarz and Blancanales. "I think these men would be mighty disappointed if there wasn't," he said.

FOR A LONG TIME after Severson and his three friends had left, the senator remained virtually motionless on the patio. Although there were three or four subsequent calls from colleagues on the Hill, he couldn't find the strength to take any of them. Then at last, painfully inching his hand across the wrought-iron table, he picked up the telephone and dialed the number of Roger Corry from the *Christian Science Monitor*.

Loosely attached to the Special Assignment's desk, Corry was said to have possessed one of the best files in Washington on the intelligence community. He was also known to have been a generally candid and willing source to those with favors to exchange. At the mention of Harwood's three visitors, however, the man could not have sounded more frigid.

"To be totally honest, Senator, I really don't think I'm in a position to help on this matter."

"I'm not asking for your help, Roger, I'm just asking if you've ever heard of them."

Silence. A distinctly cold silence.

"Okay, yes. I've heard of them."

"And?"

"And what?"

"Well who are they? What do they do?"

"Senator, I really don't think you want—"

"Look, Corry, you want me to get you an exclusive on the TRW investigation? I'll get you an exclusive. But just answer the damn question. Who are they?"

"They're professionals."

4

In all, Able Team—a covert antiterrorist squad sanctioned by the President—spent forty-eight hours probing the edges of the Domestic Insurrection Response group. Carl Lyons, Rosario Blancanales and Gadgets Schwarz examined about fifteen semiclassified CIA briefs that vaguely described the group's function. They examined thirty pages of Senate briefs that documented the group's structure. Finally, after enlisting a research team at Stony Man Farm—the Team's headquarters in the Blue Ridge mountains—they further examined forty pages of internal Pentagon traffic, which more or less delineated the group's tactical capabilities. At the end of the two-day period, however, their perception of the Wolf's Tooth unit was really no more defined than when they had begun the probe. All the men knew was that there was something out there, something big and something secret. "It's kind of like when your fishing line snags. Could be snagged on the coral, and then again it could be snagged on a great white shark," Carl Lyons had decided.

The probe was primarily conducted in one of two rented motel rooms not far from where Harwood and Severson had first met to discuss the Wolf's Tooth problem. The rooms had been reserved under the name of Anderson and were nothing if not secure. The motel, quaintly named the Sleepy Lodge, lay off the Old Mill Road three miles east of the main Shirley Memorial Highway. There was a local diner called Gracie's where the Team had their meals, and a one-room tavern called Jake's where they sometimes broke for a beer. There was also a coffee machine in the motel corridor that helped them stay awake.

On the whole, sifting through documents was frustrating, particularly for the wiry Blancanales. For although the seasoned jungle fighter appreciated the need to know one's enemy, he would have preferred a fifteen minute briefing while loading and locking an assault rifle. As it was, he found himself attempting to relieve the inaction with sets of two hundred push-ups on the shag carpet. As for the electronically minded Hermann "Gadgets" Schwarz, he primarily relieved the tension by fiddling with a passive night-vision rifle scope, which he claimed would come in handy regardless of what kind of beast they were tracking.

It was Thursday when the Team received their first real break—another crisp, clear day, with a morning frost in the trees that lingered until noon. Earlier, Lyons had FAXed a coded message to the Stony Man installation requesting a profile of all those connected with the Wolf's Tooth Complex. Stony Man researchers, under Chief Hal Brognola, had responded by establishing a link to the personnel deployment offices at Sandia and Kirtland bases. This, in turn, led to a link with what was sometimes called "The Special Index," and covered the unofficial postings of the covert teams that tended to fill the gaps between the regular Army and the intelligence community. Finally, after another five or six hours of computerized probing, Stony Man had extracted a list—thirteen names of shadowy operatives from the darkest cracks of the secret world.

It was about two o'clock in the morning. Although the sky remained clear, a wind had risen—a chill and insistent wind that smelled of the frozen earth. There was also the stench of stale coffee in the room, aftershave and cheeseburgers. In addition to the echo of the wind, there was a constant hum of television voices from the room above. Blancanales had also turned on the television but not the sound.

"What do you make of this?" Carl "Ironman" Lyons asked, passing the list of names he had just been FAXed to Blancanales.

Blancanales, otherwise known as the Politician or simply "Pol," opened a left eye.

Eight feet away, stretched out on the shag, Gadgets Schwarz also dozed.

"Class of '85," Blancanales breathed. "Class of '85 all the way."

Lyons sank onto the ugly flowered couch beside Blancanales and scanned the list over his shoulder. "What's that supposed to mean?"

"It means Central America," Schwarz murmured from the floor. "It means El Salvador, Nicaragua and half a dozen hot spots to our south."

Blancanales rose from the couch to retrieve a lukewarm cup of coffee from the table. Like the others he hadn't shaved and hadn't really slept in the last couple of days.

"Early in 1985," he said after another sip of bitter coffee. "Bill Casey and the rest of Reagan's team decide they're going to beef up the Contras with a little professional help. They're not looking for anything fancy, they just want a few dozen guys to show the natives how to blow up a power plant. Main thing is to keep it all deniable, which means they can't use the military; they want shadow warriors. They want guys on the fringe, guys who officially left the service after Nam but are still available for the special jobs."

"And by special jobs you mean?"

"Anything that's either too secret or too dirty for the regulars," Schwarz put it.

"Which, in turn, would mean anything that's against the law," Blancanales added.

Lyons picked up the list again, once more idly scanning the names. "So what does this tell us?" he asked with a yawn. "That the Wolf's Tooth unit is outside the law?"

Blancanales drained the last of his coffee, slumped to the wall and then gradually sank back down onto the carpet. "Not necessarily. It could just mean that they wanted to staff the unit with animals, a bunch guys who will do anything—no questions asked."

"Figure it this way," Schwarz said. "You want to set up a counterinsurgency group, right? And to some extent you want to man it with the meanest and toughest bastards who ever squeezed off a 9 mm round. So where are you going to turn? You're going to turn to the shadow warriors."

"Or to put it another way," Blancanales said with a finger pointing to the first name on the list, "you're going to turn to a bastard like this—Jennings Vaughan."

JENNINGS VAUGHAN was a stocky man with a face that looked like it had been carved from soapstone. The features were smooth and distinct. The nose had never been broken. The jaw was strong in contrast to the razor thin lips; and were it not for the fact that his hair was steel gray, it would have been almost impossible to place his age. As it was he still looked remarkably younger than his forty-seven years.

Like a lot of those so-called shadow warriors who inhabited the fringes of the secret world, Vaughan maintained two addresses: one in Costa Rica where a special arrangement with the local security forces kept him relatively safe from unwanted visitors, and another in Chevy Chase, Maryland, where he could stay in close touch with the various U.S.

intelligence agencies that employed him. It was rumored that he also maintained a residence in Thailand.

Vaughan's Chevy Chase residence was a nondescript, four-bedroom town house on a wooded lane adjacent to St. Catherine's School for girls. Were it not for the neighborhood, the house would have probably listed for about two hundred thousand. As it was, however, it would have probably listed for at least twice that amount. Not that Vaughan intended to sell, not at least while he still enjoyed the good graces of the intelligence community.

It was two o'clock in the afternoon when Lyons, Blancanales and Schwarz arrived at Vaughan's Chevy Chase home. Enroute in a rented Lincoln Continental, Blancanales had briefly outlined what he knew about the man. The former Black Beret had originally met Vaughan in Saigon, where Vaughan had been running one of the Phoenix program teams under what was sometimes called a special sanction.

"Which translated to mean what?" Lyons asked.

"Hunting Vietcong suspects for bounty," Schwarz replied.

"But he also had a few things going on the side," Blancanales continued.

"What kind of things?" Lyons asked.

Blancanales shrugged. "The usual. Dope, protection, prostitution. He used to run down the middle between the White Mice and the Hong Kong mafia."

"What did the Agency have to say about that?"

"Oh, they didn't give a shit...just so long as they got their piece."

After the fall of Saigon Blancanales said that he more or less lost contact with Vaughan. "Probably because he went a little dirty."

"Which means?" Lyons asked.

"That he either started feeding weapons into Cambodia or else he started working as an enforcer for one of the opium lords." As soon as things started heating up in Nicaragua, however, Jennings Vaughan was one of the first of the CIA irregulars to surface—first as a tactical adviser in the field, then as a recruitment officer in south Florida. "I also heard that he was running a little interference for Ollie North," Blancanales added, "but it may not be true."

"So what's the bottom line with this guy?" Lyons asked, easing the Lincoln to a stop beneath a spreading oak.

"The bottom line?" Blancanales repeated, gazing out through the windshield at a half-timbered house set among a grove of dwarf pines. "The bottom is, Jennings Vaughan is a team player. He may be dirty as hell in some respects, and he may talk from both sides of his mouth, but basically he's a team player. If the Pentagon asks him to jump, he'll jump. If they ask him to whack a guy, he'll whack him. And if they ask him to recruit a bunch of blood-sucking vampires for a counterinsurrection team, he'll get on the horn and start recruiting. Apart from that, however, he's a real charming fellow."

Blancanales and Schwarz left the car and moved toward the house. A Vietnamese girl answered the door. She was thin and dark, and her long, straight hair obscured half her face. There were also two young men playing pool in a room off the foyer. One of them was blond and his hair was cropped very short. The other one was dark with a rampant dragon tattooed on his left arm.

As Schwarz and Blancanales moved through the doorway and into the marble foyer, the blond peered into the hall and said, "Excuse me, but do you gentlemen have an appointment?"

Before either Schwarz or Blancanales could respond, however, a second voice echoed from the balcony above...a smooth and distinctly confident voice, with just a hint of a drawl, "That's okay, Billy, these boys don't need an appointment."

Vaughan was wearing some sort of Malaysian wrap, velveteen trousers and sandals. There was a lot of gold on his wrists and the watch was obviously worth a fortune. What initially impressed Blancanales, however, was the fact that the man hadn't changed. The face was still smooth, as if shaped from polished soapstone. The nose still hadn't been broken.

After placing an order for drinks with the girl, Vaughan led his guests into a den. It was a long and narrow room, with only one curtained window behind the desk and no direct exposure to the sunlight. The walls had been paneled with knotted pine and decorated with etchings of military aircraft: Spitfires, Zeros and a couple of P-51 Mustangs. There were also photographs of Vietnam circa 1968, three or four shots of Vaughan smiling in front of a milk bar on Tu Do and another of Vaughan in the Highlands with a wristful of gold bangles and a joint between his teeth.

"So where's the cop?" he asked, sinking into a leather chair.

Blancanales had moved to a far wall in order to examine another photograph, this one from Nicaragua. "What difference does it make?"

Vaughan shrugged. "No difference. I just thought you guys never went anywhere without Carl Lyons."

"Yeah, well Lyons is elsewhere right now," Schwarz said from the opposite corner of the room.

Vaughan's lips spread into a reptilian smile. "What happened? You boys had a little falling out?"

"Something like that," Blancanales returned.

Vaughan smiled again, this time lips spreading even wider. "Too bad. I always sort of liked the idea of knowing there was something called Able Team out there. Always made me sleep a little better, knowing you guys were out there to protect me."

The girl arrived with a tray of drinks. As she laid down the tray, Vaughan casually extended a hand and gently patted her buttocks. Her expression, however, remained unchanged.

"So what's the deal?" Vaughan asked when she had gone. "You guys on the run, on the prowl, or just looking for a little action?"

Schwarz and Blancanales took their drinks and sat down on a cold leather sofa opposite Vaughan. Above and to the left were two more photographs of barely discernible smiling faces peering out of jungle hallows. There was also the stuffed head of a jaguar, but the glass eyes were slightly askew.

"I guess you might say that we're kind of looking for a job," Blancanales asked. "I guess you might say that the Able Team thing is over and we're kind of in need of some work."

Vaughan smiled again, letting his gaze linger a moment on Blancanales. "You guys are putting me on, right?"

Schwarz was also smiling now. "Not exactly, no."

"So, what the hell happened? I thought you guys had a good thing going: traveling around the country, living in shit motels, getting paid peanuts for putting your ass on the line. What more could you want?"

"Exactly," Blancanales said. "What more could we want?"

There were echoes of music from along the corridor, whispery strains of a woman's voice singing cocktail lounge favorites. There were also noises from the pool room, the gentle click of ivory balls.

"I guess you might say that we kind of had a disagreement over procedure," Blancanales said after a long pause.

"Meaning?" Vaughan asked.

"Meaning that we popped the wrong guy and Stony Man got a little bent out of shape."

"So you guys are definitely out, that it?"

"Yeah," Schwarz said, "we're definitely out."

"And what about Lyons?"

"Lyons sided with management."

Vaughan leaned back in his chair, casually glancing through the window behind him to a leafy view of the street through the trees. Then, apparently satisfied, he slipped a hand beneath the massive teak desk and withdrew a pack of cigarettes. After lighting one he let the smoke drift through his nostrils and teeth.

"Okay," he finally said. "It just so happens that I might have something for you. A little African safari with a couple of Brits. Pay's not great, but the work's easy enough. All you got to do is tag a few natives and their Cuban advisers."

Blancanales shifted his gaze to a photograph of Vaughan smoking another cigarette in the shadow of the Lincoln Memorial. "Actually," the Able Team commando said at last, "we were kind of hoping you might have something a little closer to home. Maybe something out west at a place called the Wolf's Tooth."

Although Vaughan's eyes may have narrowed slightly, there was no other discernible change in his expression. "Who told you about the Wolf's Tooth, Pol?"

"Let's just say that word gets around," Schwarz replied.

"Yeah, well not that kind of word. So who told you?"

"Saw it on one of the Stony Man internals," Blancanales said. "It mentioned that you were doing some recruiting for a unit out there, that the pay was good and the long-term benefits even better."

Vaughan took another drag on his cigarette, letting the smoke seep out from his teeth again. "Wolf's Tooth is a military operation. They're not looking for hired guns."

"That's not what we heard," Schwarz replied. "We heard they were looking for people to handle the stuff that was a little too dirty for the regulars...which is kind of our speciality."

Vaughan bit his lower lip and shifted his gaze from Schwarz to Blancanales.

"All right, why don't you tell me what kind of arrangement you had in mind?"

Blancanales shrugged. "We're easy. They need a trainer? We'll train. They need some deniable muscle? We'll start flexing. We're real easy."

Vaughan took another slow drag from the cigarette, this time spraying the ceiling with smoke. "The Wolf's Tooth program isn't just another job," he said at last. "It's a cause. You understand what I'm saying? It's a cause."

Schwarz lumped up his mouth for a quick, hard grin. "Well, it just so happens that we've been looking for a cause."

This time, however, Vaughan did not return the smile. "Hey, I'm not kidding here. The Wolf's Tooth program isn't just another job. It's something to believe in, something to fight for. Now, if you guys are just looking for a quick fifteen grand, then I suggest you try the African safari. But if you're serious about making a commitment, real serious, then I might be able to put you in touch with some people."

"When?" Blancanales asked.

Vaughan glanced at the telephone, then at his Cartier wristwatch. "Right now," he replied. "I can probably put you in touch with some people right now."

Instead of reaching for the telephone, however, Vaughan slipped his hand into the desk and withdrew a Beretta automatic.

"But first," he said, "you've got to fill out a job application."

Blancanales calculated the distance, while Schwarz tried to estimate how long it would take him to withdraw his modified .45 auto from the holster beneath his jacket. In the end, however, neither man was particularly happy with the results of their calculation...so they simply remained seated, watching, waiting, listening.

"First question," Vaughan said, resting the butt of the weapon on the desk. "Where did you *really* hear about the Wolf's Tooth program?"

Blancanales cocked his head with a slightly bored sigh. "Like we told you, it was mentioned in one of Stony Man cables."

"What kind of cable?"

"Internal."

"What was the source?"

"I can't remember. Pentagon, I think. Maybe CIA."

"What did it say?"

"Not much. Just that the military was staffing a base out west to deal with possible domestic problems, and they were looking for a few irregulars to take care of stuff that the military couldn't touch."

"And my name was mentioned?"

Blancanales nodded. "That's right. Your name was mentioned as an outside recruiter."

Vaughan cocked his head with a thoughtful frown, then reached across the desk with his left hand and spoke softly into an intercom. "Billy. Larry. Come on in here for a moment. And bring your pool cue." Then turning back to Schwarz and Blancanales, "Sorry about this boys, but I happen to know that you're lying."

Once again Blancanales began to calculate the distance between his right hand and that Beretta. Concurrently, Schwarz began to rethink drawing his .45 auto from beneath his windbreaker. Before either man could even begin to make a move, however, Vaughan's two associates appeared in the doorway: one of them carrying a shortened pool cue, the other dangling two pair of handcuffs.

"Now, this is the way we're going to play it," Vaughan said as he rose from the chair behind the desk and leveled the Beretta at Blancanales's chest. "I'm going to ask the questions, and you boys are going to supply the answers. Every time you fail to answer or answer with a lie, Billy and Larry here are going to club you with that pool stick. Now stand up, turn around, and put your hands behind your back."

Several things went through Blancanales's mind as he slowly rose to his feet. He thought about a time in Little Havana when he had dropped a two-hundred-and-fifty-pound bouncer with a blind rear kick to the gut. He thought about a time in San Antonio when he had pasted two Cuban middleweights with a back-knuckle combination. He thought about Vaughan's Beretta and wondered whether it was loaded with Olin Super or merely one of the new subsonics.

At precisely the same moment Schwarz was also thinking about the Beretta's load—wondering if Billy's body was bulky enough to stop a slug, and if so, was he quick enough to pull the crew-cut punk into the line of fire before Vaughan could squeeze the trigger.

Before either man could translate these thoughts into action, however, the windowpane behind Vaughan's shoulder exploded with a shower of glass and the sudden appearance of Carl Lyons screaming from behind a Smith & Wesson, *"Freeze!"*

Vaughan responded first, whirling in his chair and leveling the Beretta. Before he could squeeze off a shot, however, Blancanales was on him like a clawing cat—lunging across the polished teak, locking Vaughan's arm at the elbow and jamming it down to the breaking point. Vaughan grunted in agonized pain and frantically struck back with a tiger's claw. But before he could connect, Blancanales hit him again—two quick shots with a whipping back-knuckle.

Larry, stepping back for a little distance, then stepped in with the pool cue. But before he could bring it into play, Schwarz snap-kicked a quick, hard shot to the groin that left Larry doubled up in blinding pain. Then as part of the same phenomenally fast movement, Schwarz turned and withdrew his .45 auto and pressed the muzzle into the blond kid's throat saying, "Why don't you do yourself a favor, Billy, and save your life? Hmm?"

Vaughan, obviously, decided he'd also take Schwarz's advice. After struggling for only another second or two, he simply went limp, dropping the Beretta and grinning, "Okay, Pol. I got the point. I got the point!"

The telephones were ripped from the jacks. Billy and Larry were handcuffed to the pool table. The little Oriental girl was locked in the bathroom with a diet soda and copy of *Vogue*. Vaughan was pressed back into his deep leather chair in order to face Able Team.

"So, you're the cop," Vaughan said, shifting in his chair to get a good look at Lyons.

Lyons smirked, raised his .45 as if to whip the muzzle across Vaughan's face but then apparently decided against it.

In addition to fragments of glass and traces of blood, Vaughan had also spilled his drink on the rug...which he seemed to find amusing. "Can't invite you guys anywhere." He smiled, glancing at the reddish stain.

"It's kind of like this," Blancanales said from the corner. "We're going to ask the questions, and you're going to supply the answers. If you fail to—"

But Vaughan's smile widened, "Give me a break, will you? You guys don't even know what you're dealing with here. You don't even have a clue."

Schwarz had used a screwdriver to crack the lock on a filing cabinet. In the folder marked Wolf's Tooth, there were only photographs: six eight-by-ten glossies of occasional players from the shadow wars. He also found more than ten thousand dollars in a buff envelope.

"We're not out for blood," Lyons said softly, hunkering down to the beige rug beside Vaughan's chair. "We just want to find out what's going on."

Jennings Vaughan merely grinned. "No, you don't. You don't want to hear anything about this. Believe me."

"It's like this," Blancanales said. "We know that somebody named Harold Gibb tried to blow the whistle on what's been going down out there. We also know that he may have gotten wasted for his trouble, probably by the same team that tried to pop the senator."

"Screw the senator," Vaughan said. "The senator's a wimp. He's a Commie kissing wimp, who'd sell this nation for thirty bucks and a pat on the back."

Ignoring the comment Lyons leaned a little closer to Vaughan's left ear. "So what's the deal out there, Jennings? What's the Wolf's Tooth all about?"

Vaughan laughed again. "Hope," he said. "It's about hope. It's about the hope of saving this nation from the wimps and traitors who are trying to flush us down the toilet."

"And where do you fit in?"

"Like the man said, I'm the talent scout. I'm the guy who finds the chosen few to fill the ranks of the chosen elite. Which you boys might have qualified for, if you hadn't turned out to be such ass-kissing fools."

"So who's your boss?" Blancanales asked from the other side of Vaughan's chair. "Who signs your checks?"

Vaughan smirked and shook his head. "Hey, who do you think you're dealing with here? You think I'm going to tell you something like that? You're crazy. Besides, the guy I deal with isn't a player. He's just an errand boy. You want to find out who the players are, you got to go to the top."

"And where's the top?" Lyons asked. "Pentagon?"

"That's right the Pentagon...and a few like-minded people in other places."

"What places?" Blancanales asked.

But Vaughan shook his head, pressed a fist to his mouth, then sank a little deeper into the leather with another thin smile.

"You guys still don't get it, do you?" he said. "The Wolf's Tooth isn't just another screen pass. It's an end-run sweep. It's the game breaker and nobody is going to stop it. Believe me."

"So who's making the plays, Vaughan," Lyons whispered. "Huh? Who's calling plays?"

"Hey, give me a break. I'm just the water boy. I don't know things like that."

"But you know how to find out, don't you?"

Again Vaughan just shook his head and smirked. "Screw you, Lyons. Screw you."

Lyons rose from the rug and moved to the window. Earlier Blancanales had whispered in his ear, "Let me sweat the bastard," but Lyons had ignored it. Schwarz had also offered to lend a helping fist, but Lyons had settled on an alternative route.

"All right, this is the deal," he said to Vaughan softly. "You're going to call your contact and tell him that you've got three more recruits for the Wolf's Tooth unit—three mean mothers who'll do anything that's required... *anything*."

Vaughan slowly shifted his gaze until his eyes met Lyons's eyes. "You got to be kidding, right?"

"You might also say that our speciality is urban action, down-and-dirty urban action, and that we've got tricks that the regular Army instructors never even dreamed of."

Vaughan wrinkled his nose as if in response to a foul stench. "You definitely got to be kidding. Anyway, I just got through recruiting a couple of instructors, a couple of mean old boys out of Houston to teach a special course on crowd control."

"Well, then maybe those two boys from Houston just didn't work out. Maybe they got a better offer from the Africans and maybe we're just going to have be their replacements. Understand what I'm saying?"

For a moment Vaughan seemed entirely unable to respond—perspiration beaded across his forehead and his hands knotted into fists.

"Look, even if I wanted to get you guys in there, I still couldn't take the chance that—"

Lyons cut him off with a quick shake of the head. "I'm not asking for a favor, Vaughan. I'm telling you the way it's going to be. You're going to make that call and get us into the compound and that's all there is to it."

Vaughan bit his lips, fixing his eyes on the stain at his feet. "All right." He finally sighed. "But it's going to take a little while. I mean I can't just—"

"You've got two hours, and we'll be sitting here with you the whole time."

JENNINGS VAUGHAN had to place three phone calls in order to arrange Able Team's placement in the Wolf's Tooth unit. He had to place two calls to a remote exchange in Virginia and a third to a Navy chief petty officer named Terry Stockton. Half an hour later Vaughan received an incoming call from a Pentagon research and planning assistant, whom Vaughan knew only as the Hacker.

This call lasted exactly four minutes. The Hacker, who sounded like a middle-aged white male, asked what it was that Vaughan wanted. Vaughan replied that he was having a little trouble locating his "Houston Team" and wanted to scrap them for three local guys.

"They any good?" the Hacker asked.

"You kidding?" Vaughan replied. "These guys are the best, absolutely the best."

"And you trust them?"

Vaughan glanced up from his desk into the barrel of Schwarz's automatic. "With my life," he said.

"All right," the Hacker replied. "Send them on out at the end of the week, but don't tell them anything more than they need to know."

Following these phone calls, Lyons placed a call to Stony Man Farm. He spoke to Hal Brognola, regarding the use of a van and a couple of boys from internal security, "to transport and hold three males and one female." He also passed on the names and numbers of Vaughan's Pentagon contacts.

"Hold them for how long?" Brognola asked.

"For as long as it takes," Lyons replied.

He hung up the phone and turned to Vaughan. "It's not that we don't trust you," he said. "It's just that we'll feel a little better if you spend the next few days in the cooler."

"What are you talking about?" Vaughan replied. "I did what you told me to do, didn't I?"

"And as a reward we're going to send you and your friends on a little holiday, just until we find out what your employers have going in New Mexico," Blancanales chuckled.

5

For days after witnessing Harold Gibb's death, Molly Meekin had found herself thinking of the little things. She recalled that the blue-eyed soldier's breath had smelled faintly of mints, and that they had blindfolded her with some sort an elastic headband. She recalled that the handcuffs had pinched her wrists but that she had been too frightened to complain. She knew that the man that had actually done the shooting was from either West Virginia or Kentucky, and that the blue-eyed soldier sounded a little like her cousin Nick after he had returned from New York where he had taken acting lessons. Finally, she had also been certain that they had taken her back into the hills, probably to that secret base on the mesa.

"Now you just take it real easy," the blue-eyed soldier had said when he had led her into the windowless Quonset hut, uncuffed her wrists and removed the blindfold. "You just lie down over there on that cot, make yourself comfy and take it real easy. And don't you worry your pretty little head about a thing, because you'll be out of here before you know it."

Before leaving her under the light of a naked bulb, he also took her wristwatch.

For a long time she had mainly been conscious of the sounds—the rain pounding on the corrugated roof, the wind whistling through a slit in the cinder block walls, the occasional echo of rumbling trucks and the steady throb of generators.

Finally, Molly became preoccupied with her immediate safety. She worried about rape, murder and torture. She couldn't keep herself from recalling a sequence from a film that had shown a woman being strapped to an operating table and then injected with battery acid. She also recalled reading about electrical abuse in Brazil and Argentina and how the Nazis disemboweled their prisoners and then cauterized the wounds so that death would come very slowly. But gradually she began to make a much more rational assessment of her predicament.

To begin with, she turned her attention to her physical surroundings. Apart from the cot, a card table and two folding chairs, the room was virtually bare. There was, however, a toilet and a cramped shower stall, and she had found a supply of blankets and towels in a footlocker. Although the door and walls were impenetrable, she doubted that the hut had been constructed to hold prisoners. Which presumably meant that she was a special case, an accident.

Next, she turned her attention to the sounds outside. When the rain had finally subsided, for example, she began to hear voices: someone shouting something about an armored personnel carrier, someone else calling about a microwave relay. Then there had been the sound of incoming choppers and indistinct voices over loudspeakers.

Finally she had worked up enough courage to peek through the narrow slit below the ceiling. In order to accomplish the task, she had to set the chair precariously on the table and then slowly pull herself up by means of the air-conditioning unit. The view was still fairly restricted because of the walls of adjacent huts and a nest of radio antennae, but she knew immediately that she was being held at some sort of military base. It definitely lay on the mesa and probably stretched three miles to the far northern hills. There were barracks for at least six or seven hundred men and the visible hardware included four tanks and two transport aircraft.

IT WAS SIX OR SEVEN O'CLOCK one morning when two men finally came to see her. The older one was tall and thin, with a rather distinguished head of snow white hair and finely chiseled features. The younger one was muscular and dark, with a neat moustache. They were both dressed in starched khaki uniforms with short-sleeve shirts and immaculately pressed trousers. The younger one carried a clipboard and remained standing by the door. The older one pulled up a folding chair and faced her from across the card table. She, in turn, met his gaze from the corner of the cot.

"Miss Meekin," the older man said with an oddly paternal smile.

But because she couldn't tell whether it was a question or a statement, she said nothing. It did cross her mind that they probably got her name from her driver's license ... which meant that they also knew where she lived, where she was born and where she went to school.

"My name is Colonel William T. Stack," the older one continued. "This gentleman is Corporal Harris. We would like to formally welcome you to this installation and apologize for any inconvenience you may have been caused."

Then although she muttered some kind of acknowledgment, she basically just kept staring ... not sure what her reaction should be.

"Now, the first thing we'd like to clear up are the circumstances of your arrival here. So if you could just give me some idea as to where you were going that night ...?"

"Where I was going?"

"That's right. Where you were going with a wanted fugitive from this command."

She shook her head in disbelief and shifted her gaze to the corporal by the door—his pen poised above the clipboard in anticipation of her answer.

"I wasn't . . . I wasn't going anywhere with him. I just picked him up along the road and was giving him a ride to a phone."

"A telephone?"

"That's right. I was just taking him to a telephone."

"Why?"

She took a deep breath, rolling her eyes to the ceiling. "Because he said he needed to make a phone call."

"And you had never seen him before?"

"No."

"Then why did you stop and pick him up?"

She shook her head again. "Because he looked like he was in trouble."

"He looked like he was in trouble?"

"That's right. He looked like he might have been hurt or something."

"So you pulled over to the side of the road and asked him if he needed a ride?"

"Exactly."

"And what did he say?"

"He said that he'd been in an accident and asked if I'd give him a lift to the highway."

"So that he could make a phone call?"

"That's right. So he could make a phone call."

"Did he tell you who it was that he wanted to call?"

"No, not really. He just said something about the Automobile Club, about wanting to call the Automobile Club because he'd been in an accident."

"But he didn't mention any names?"

"No."

There was a brief silence, while the colonel exchanged a quick glance with the corporal, and the corporal apparently checked something on the clipboard.

"What else did you and the fugitive talk about?" the colonel finally asked.

She shrugged, suddenly growing very frightened without quite knowing why. "Nothing," she said.

"Nothing? You mean to say that you rode with the fugitive for more than twenty minutes, and you didn't talk about anything?"

"Well, maybe I asked him if he was from this base."

"And how did you know about this base?"

"Everybody knows. It's even been in the newspapers."

"So how did he respond to the question?"

"He just said yes."

"You mean, yes he was from this base?"

"That's right."

"Anything else?"

"Not really."

"Are you absolutely sure?"

She took another deep breath and then briefly shut her eyes. "Maybe I also asked him what kind of stuff was going on up here."

"And how did he respond to that question?"

She shook her head, briefly recalling Gibb's empty gaze and tired voice. "He didn't."

Again there was a momentary silence while the colonel and corporal exchanged knowing glances. Then finally turning to face her again, the colonel said only, "Well, that will be all for now, Miss Meekin."

She held the gaze for a full two seconds. "What do you mean, that will be all?"

"I mean that we have no further questions for you at this time."

"So I can go?"

He rose from his chair and moved to the door. "No, I'm afraid not."

"But you can't just keep me here. I mean . . . I mean you just can't do it. My family will be looking for me."

"I'm sorry."

"You're sorry? What do you mean you're sorry? That boy was shot. Now you're holding me prisoner and all you can say is you're sorry?" She glanced at the walls, glanced at her hands. Then finally letting it all out in a harsh shout, "Look, I demand to be released right now! Do you understand? I demand to be released right now!"

But again the colonel only smiled. "I'm sorry."

6

For the first three days of her confinement, Molly continued to worry about getting shot, raped or tortured. Then little by little, as one uneventful hour ate up another, she began to turn her thoughts to the bigger questions...like what the hell was really going on out here?

She considered the possibility that she had walked into the middle of an espionage case. That by having picked up that staff sergeant on the Wolf's Tooth road, she had inadvertently aided and abetted a major Soviet spy. Her confinement was therefore based on a simple case of mistaken intentions. Although she thought she had merely been helping a roadside victim, Colonel Stack and company believed that she was a Russian agent.

After further thought, however, she decided that this theory was extremely unlikely. For one thing, the military had no legal jurisdiction over civilian offenders except in a state of national emergency. Even if they did believe that she was some sort of spy, they would have had to turn her over to the Justice Department for proper arrest and arraignment.

After noting the inordinate amount of hardware around the camp, it occurred to her that maybe she had stumbled on some sort of supersecret military operation—perhaps the departure point for a hostage rescue mission. Therefore, although clearly illegal, the base commander had decided that he had no alternative but to confine her so that she wouldn't inadvertently compromise the mission and thereby endanger the lives of his men.

She eventually decided that this theory just didn't hold any water, either.

Finally, after noting the continual echoes of gunfire from what was probably a practice range and the rumble of armored vehicles from the far ends of the mesa, she began to devise a third and altogether more chilling scenario: what if Wolf's Tooth compound was some type of renegade outfit? What if they were operating totally outside the law, totally beyond the knowledge and authority of regular military channels?

COLONEL STACK RETURNED at the end of the third day. He was accompanied by Corporal Harris and arrived just as she had finished as much as she could eat of a chicken dinner, which had been served on a steel plate, delivered by a silent private. Stack took one look at her half-eaten meal and looked up at her. "If you're unhappy with the food, Miss Meekin, I'm sure we can make other arrangements. All you have to do is ask."

By this point, she was too frightened to even stare back at him.

He once again faced her from across the card table, while she remained huddled on a corner of the cot. The corporal remained by the door with his clipboard. Although the colonel's demeanor seemed somewhat more casual, she was certain that his questions had been prepared in advance.

"I just want to go over a few more details regarding your encounter with the fugitive," he said.

She didn't respond, didn't even look at him, but she could feel his eyes boring into her.

"You mentioned that he admitted having been stationed at this installation, correct?"

She tried to form her lips into a reply but couldn't seem to manage it.

"I asked if the fugitive happened to mention that he was stationed at this installation, Miss Meekin."

She took a deep breath, clenching her left fist under the blanket. "Yes," she finally whispered. "He told me that he was stationed at this installation."

"In what capacity?"

She shook her head again. "I don't think I understand what—"

"Did he tell you what he did here?"

"No."

"Are you sure?"

"Yes."

"He gave you no indication at all what his duties were?"

She shrugged. "All he told me was—"

"All he told you was what? All he told you was what, Miss Meekin?"

"All he told me was that he was kind of playing it down the middle."

"Playing it down the middle? What did he mean by that?"

"I asked him what was going on up here. I asked him whether they were planning for World War III or just trying to keep the peace, and he said they were just kind of playing it down the middle."

"And what do you suppose he was implying by that?"

She shrugged again. "I don't know. I guess he meant..." She broke off with another shake of her head.

"You guess he meant what, Miss Meekin? What?"

"I guess he meant that maybe there was some kind of secret plan to—"

"To what, Miss Meekin? You guess that there was some kind of secret plan to do what?"

"To take control in case of an emergency. To take control of the population in case of a national emergency."

The colonel dropped his gaze to her half-eaten meal, then gradually shifted his eyes back to the corporal by the door. Earlier she'd heard idling trucks in the yard and hollow voices over shortwave radios and she suddenly realized that it was very quiet. The silence was chilling; it spread from the pit of her stomach and left her numb, trembling and more terrified than she had ever thought possible....

Finally she couldn't keep herself from shouting, "Look, I don't know anything, all right! I don't know anything at all! So why don't you just let me go? Okay? Why don't you just let me go?"

The colonel looked at her, passed a tired hand across his mouth, then slowly rose to his feet. "As I said, Miss Meekin, if you're unhappy with your food, I'm sure we can get you something else."

THERE WAS MORE SHOOTING that night from the far south rim of the mesa. It began with sporadic rifle fire but quickly graduated to heavier artillery: mortars or cannons, rockets and grenades. There were also sounds of helicopters, dozens of them hovering high above. At one point she even heard what sounded like women and children, a hundred frantic women and children falling under a hail of bullets. Eventually Molly realized that the screams were coming from the public address system and were probably just a recording intended to enhance the realism.

But the realism of what?

An all out attack on a civilian population?

7

Lyle Severson laid the fruits of his investigation on Senator Harwood's desk: four typewritten pages of detailed information. In all he had spent six days gathering the material. Some of it had been gleaned from internal memos, some of it from National Security estimates and some of it from seemingly casual conversations with friends and acquaintances in and around the intelligence community. On the whole, his findings were rather like an advertisement for a soon-to-be released horror film. Even though one couldn't be entirely certain what the movie was about, it was obvious that the thing was going to be scary.

"I suppose we'd better talk about security," Severson said. "About making sure that none of us gets killed before we get a chance to unravel this thing."

Harwood shifted in his chair to relieve the pressure on his left hip. Although his recovery had been fairly rapid, he was still wearing the cast and still suffered from occasional headaches and aching ribs.

"What do you have in mind?" the senator asked.

Severson shifted his gaze to the window. "Well, the first thing is to get you out of here and into a safehouse," he said.

Harwood responded with a quizzical frown. "Do you really think that's necessary?"

"I don't know," Severson replied with a quick nod at Harwood's leg and the foam collar around his neck. "What do you think? You think maybe somebody's after your ass, or what?"

Harwood's aged housekeeper appeared with coffee and croissants, butter and honey. The day outside was chilly, but Harwood's little garden den could not have been more comfortable, what with a smoldering fire in the grate and the partially obscured view of winter roses.

"Look, why don't you just give me the bottom line?" Harwood said as he reached for a coffee cup and cream. "Why don't you tell me exactly what it is we're facing here?"

Severson tore off the end of a croissant, popped it in his mouth, and then continued staring at the window. "The bottom line, huh?"

"I mean assuming the worst, what exactly are we looking at?" Harwood added.

Again, however, Severson merely shook his head. "I'm not sure," he said after a long pause. "I suppose it's possible that the Wolf's Tooth is strictly on the level, operating under a secret Presidential mandate. But that doesn't exactly explain why somebody tried to run you into the swamp."

"Then what?"

"Well, I'm afraid that I'd have to say that it's renegade. I'd have to say that someone or some group has basically taken it upon themselves to form their own little army."

"Why?"

"I'm not sure. Could be that they want a strike force to handle the Central American problem once and for all. Or...."

"Or what, Lyle?"

"Or perhaps they're planning to use the Wolf's Tooth unit to handle a problem a little further to the north."

Harwood had carefully buttered the end of his croissant, but suddenly he couldn't seem to bring himself to eat it. He also hadn't touched his coffee or the wedge of French cheese.

"Maybe you'd better run that by me again," he said at last.

Severson nodded. "This is just a working theory, all right? It's just one scenario suggested by the facts. But the truth is, I think we have to face the fact that the Wolf's Tooth unit was originally designed as a domestic control force."

"And by domestic control you mean?"

"I mean total civilian and governmental control."

There were echoes of a ringing telephone, then the modulated voice of the housekeeper explaining to someone that the senator could not be disturbed. Meanwhile Harwood had grown very still again, his hands dangling over the edge of his rocker, his jaw slack and his eyes fixed straight ahead.

"Look at it this way," Severson continued. "What do they do up at the Wolf's Tooth? They play games, right? They set up war game models and then work all the options. A dozen terrorist teams, supported by a few thousand radicals take over New York City. What are you going to do about it? What are your choices—war games."

"And just before Harold Gibb vanished, he said that they weren't playing games. I mean that was the gist of his message: they're not playing games at the Wolf's Tooth."

"Exactly," Severson breathed.

Harwood slowly rose from his chair and limped to the window. "Why?" he whispered. "I mean it's not as if the Republicans haven't given the Pentagon virtually everything they've asked for—the Stealth, Star Wars, the MX and God knows what else. So why?"

"Because like everyone else in this damn town, they want more. Besides, it probably proved to be just too irresistible. They saw that the opportunity for a total military takeover was both clear and present, and they obviously just couldn't resist going for it."

"So then what the hell do we do about it?"

"Well, for one thing we don't start crying wolf. We do that, and they'll just slip back into their holes and wait for another day. Or worse, they'll move up the timetable and blow us all to hell. So for starters I want you to play it very cool. I want you to keep your head down and play it very, very cool. Do not try to contact your people on the Hill. Do not leak it to Jack Anderson."

"How do you suggest I handle my calendar?"

"Hey, you've just been in a terrible accident. People are going to expect you to spend a few days in the country for a little rest and relaxation."

"What about my committee work? I can't just vanish, and leave the committee."

"We'll work something out. The important thing is for you to stay alive while we determine exactly what their game plan is, how they intend to grab the ball and when."

"And just how do you intend to determine that?"

Severson finally took a sip of coffee, but when he realized it was cold he put the cup aside. "Well, that's where Able Team comes in," he said. "That's why I brought them into the game."

Harwood moved away from the window and ran a finger along the spine of a book on his shelf.

"You're only talking about three men, Lyle," Harwood said at last. "Okay, so they may be tough, but there's only three of them."

Severson shrugged. "Something tells me that's not going to be the problem."

"And how do you know you can trust them? I mean after all, they're essentially from the same pool as the Wolf's Tooth recruits. Ex-Special Forces. Ex-Vietnam...same basic background."

"That may be true," Severson agreed, "but on the other hand they're not team players. They don't particularly like the Pentagon brass and they definitely don't trust the radical fringe. Besides, while they may occasionally bend the rules a little, they still believe in preserving the Bill of Rights...which, I might add, just happens to be what this game is all about."

They parted in the garden among the winter roses. Enroute from the study Severson had withdrawn a pair of binoculars in order to scan the lane below. He was also armed with a snub-nosed Colt revolver.

"By the way," Harwood said suddenly. "I don't know if this is even related, but one of my aides picked up an interesting little footnote from a friend in the Bureau."

"What's that?" Severson asked, as he continued scanning the ranks of parked cars and the gently shifting shadows beneath the far pines.

"It seems that the local New Mexico office reported a missing person the other night—a girl."

Severson shifted his magnified gaze to a Ford van with blackened windows and too much antennae. "So?"

"So she was last known to be driving in the area of the Wolf's Tooth mesa. Also, the dates correspond. According to the SAC report, she vanished just about the same time that Staff Sergeant Gibb disappeared."

"And you think there's a connection?"

"I think it's possible, yes."

"So what are you suggesting?"

Harwood squinted at the lane below, trying to remember which cars belonged to neighbors and which ones he had never seen before.

"Maybe you could mention it to Lyons and company," he said. "Tell them to keep their eyes open for a pretty little nineteen-year-old by the name of Molly Meekin."

Severson lowered his binoculars, finally satisfied that the van was just a van and that the shadows were just shadows shifting in the icy breeze.

"John, I can appreciate your concern for this girl, but I kind of get the feeling that Lyons and his people are going to have their hands full just trying to stay alive out there. You understand what I'm telling you? I just don't think we're in the position right now to start concerning ourselves with any one individual case."

Harwood smiled, gently laying a hand on Severson's shoulder. "Hey, I thought you said that what we're doing here is trying to preserve the Bill of Rights?"

"I did, but under the circumstances—"

"Well, isn't that what the Bill of Rights is all about, Lyle? Preserving the life and liberty of individuals like Molly Meekin? Hmm? Isn't that what it's all about?"

8

From the air the Wolf's Tooth mesa looked a little like a dinosaur's skull—the ancient alluvial deposits like vertebrae with a gray cap of sandy rock above. There was white pine along the northern rim and spruce to the south, though it was generally a barren place of desert willows and creosote bush. The winter nights were cold, occasionally freezing. The days were also dry and cold. Legend said it was a place of spirits, furious Pueblo spirits that were often heard singing like coyotes in the wind.

It was late Friday afternoon when Lyons, Schwarz and Blancanales reached the mesa. Enroute from the adjacent airstrip at Kirtland, Lyons counted seven armored assault vehicles and three ATVs fitted with 50-caliber machine guns. Judging from the tracks in the dung-colored earth, there may have also been tanks but he couldn't be certain. Upon reaching the main compound, they were met by a beefy sergeant named Collier.

"I don't know what you boys might have heard about this place, but figure that most of it isn't true," the sergeant said.

Able Team was then escorted to their quarters—a stark Quonset hut, with little more than three cots, three footlockers and a space heater. While conducting an innocuous conversation concerning the weather, Schwarz proceeded to inspect the room for hidden microphones. Finally satisfied that the place was reasonably clean, he stretched out on the cot for a quick nap. Lyons and Blancanales, also exhausted from the six-hour flight and the two-hour wait in a steel hut, still couldn't bring themselves to rest.

"I don't suppose you've got any real plan in mind," Blancanales said at last.

Lyons shrugged, shifting his gaze past the drab green walls to the equally drab vision of the campgrounds beyond the dusty window. "I figure we'd just sort of play it by ear," he replied. "Get to know the place. Get to know the people. Maybe shake the tree a little and see what falls."

Blancanales was also gazing out that dusty window to a brown view of barracks, chain link and pavement. What might have been exploding shells in the distance, however, was probably just rising dust.

"I've got to tell you something," he finally sighed. "We're not dealing with just another bunch of grunts here."

Lyons also sighed. "Sure."

"Hey, I'm serious, Carl. These guys are good. These guys have been around the block. You slip up with these guys, and they'll cut you to pieces."

Lyons sighed again. "Yeah, well I don't intend to slip up," he said.

AT PRECISELY five o'clock the sergeant returned with a summons from Colonel William T. Stack. Thirteen minutes later they found themselves in an oblong briefing room at the southern end of the compound. Sixteen folding chairs had been arranged in four rows across the gray linoleum. The corrugated walls were bare, except for two topographical maps of the surrounding terrain. Just inside the door, however, there were two somewhat more personal photographs of the Reagan-Bush team and a grainy photograph of Stack in Saigon circa 1969.

Stack reminded Blancanales of many colonels he had known in Vietnam: lean, hard and continually working his jaw. He tended to speak in short, clipped sentences while his gaze remained fixed on your forehead. He obviously spent a long time grooming his moustache and had probably had a tattoo removed from his wrist. He had also seen a fair amount of combat; it was in his eyes. It was in the way he walked into the room, planted himself in front of the podium and began to spit out his briefing as if there were no tomorrow.

"Technically, gentlemen, this group is a direct descendant of Colonel Charlie Beckwith's 1st Special Forces Operations Detachment at Fort Bragg, more commonly known as Delta Force. Like that unit, we comprise approximately three hundred able-bodied souls, to be further divided into sixteen units should circumstances call for it. Also like that unit, we are answerable to Joint Special Operations Command, the 1st Special Forces Group and the Secretary of Defense. Unlike that unit, however, we are directed by a Pentagon board for low intensity conflict."

Next there were visual aids: crude black-and-white diagrams to indicate the command lines, a blue-and-black flow chart to indicate the budgetary channels. It was at this point that Stack began to outline the primary directives, including the development of special tactics and training programs to implement those tactics. "Which is where you gentlemen come in," he added. "Special tactical instruction."

He slid onto a corner of the rectangular table, as if to emphasize the fact that the briefing had ended and there was now to be an informal discussion.

"Although I have not been specifically apprised of your skills," he continued, "I think I've got a pretty fair idea of what you boys do for a living. So, if it's all the same to you, maybe we should just lay our cards on the table. My men happen to be the meanest bunch of soldiers this side of Moscow, but they do not necessarily possess every trick in the book. They also do not have your practical experience in the field. By the same token, though, I think you'll find that you're not exactly dealing with raw meat...if you know what I mean?''

Lyons eased back into his chair and casually stretched his legs. ''Well, if you could give us a little idea as to what kind of activities you anticipate...''

Stack responded with a curt nod. ''Basically we're looking at three possible scenarios: massive terrorist infiltration, spontaneous domestic uprising and hostile population control.''

''On what sort of terrain?''

''Primarily urban.''

''Armed with what?''

''You name it, they'll have it.''

''And you're training program to date?''

''Three phases, lasting thirty-two weeks, and covering all aspects of combat intensity. We also rough 'em up a little to give them an idea of what they could face if they fall into enemy hands.''

Lyons exchanged a quick glance with Blancanales, then another with Schwarz. Finally taking a long and slow breath, he said, ''What about your hand-to-hand program?''

Stack allowed himself a thin smile. ''Oh, I think you'll find that my men are already well versed in that area, Mr. Lyons.''

Lyons also smiled. ''Well, we'll just have to see about that, won't we?''

IT BEGAN the following morning at half past seven. In all
there were sixty-five men in attendance, including Stack and
Corporal Harris. Lyons and Blancanales faced the men
from the edge of a paved quadrangle, while Schwarz
watched from the perimeter. Fifteen square feet of canvas
mat had been laid to minimize injuries. Despite the post-
dawn chill, Lyons wore only a pair of gray sweats and a T-
shirt. Among the training aids were three fully automatic
Uzis, four dummy grenades and an assortment of Ka-bar
survival knives.

Lyons began with a fairly classic introduction. "Regardless of how well armed you may be, there will undoubtedly
come a point when you will have to rely on your hands and
feet in order to save your life. If you do not possess the necessary hand and foot skills, you will die. It's that simple."

Then slowly shifting his gaze along the ranks of seated
men, he asked for a volunteer.

There was a momentary hush as several of the men seated
below exchanged nervous glances. Finally, with soft mur-
murs of approval, a lean corporal stood up and approached
the mat. A dark and muscular man, he moved with catlike
agility. The intensity of his eyes further suggested that he
was probably the best that this unit could offer in the way
of an unarmed combatant and was thus obviously intended
as a test of Lyons's own ability.

"What's your name, corporal?" Lyons asked with a distinctly casual smile.

"Hicks," the boy drawled.

"Well, Corporal Hicks, how about you showing me what
you know?"

The corporal returned the smile with a slight nod, slipped
off his shoes and stepped onto the mat. Although by this
point Lyons no longer had any doubt that the boy was
trained, he still continued to maintain his easy noncha-

lance...glancing back to Blancanales with a grin, then sliding his gaze to Stack.

"Tell you what we'll do, Corporal," Lyons said as he joined the boy on the mat. "I want you to pretend that I'm the worst shit you've ever encountered. I want you to pretend that I've just raped your grandmother and eaten your baby. I want you to get all that real firm in your mind and then come at me with everything you've got. You understand?"

"Yes, sir," Hicks replied as he gently lowered himself into a stance. "I understand perfectly."

Obviously a practitioner of an Okinawan style, the boy opened with a quick feint to the head and then a skipping snap-kick to the groin. Having read the movement in advance, however, Lyons merely sidestepped with another smile. The boy's next move consisted of a wheel-kick and a spinning-rear combination, followed by a back-knuckle to the face. Again, however, the boy's power surge acted as a telegraph and Lyons easily sidestepped the blows.

If nothing else, the boy was fast—very fast on his feet and very fast with his hands. Thus, in order to avoid the humiliation of a useless strike, Lyons decided that he probably had to employ what he had hoped to save for last: the advanced striking technique.

Supposedly refined by Bruce Lee but based upon far more arcane and ancient *Shao-lin* tenets, the advanced striking technique employed an exceptionally simple maxim: the strike that cannot be blocked is the strike that cannot be anticipated; and the strike that cannot be anticipated is the strike that begins with nothing.

To initiate the strike Lyons set himself in a casual stance— the feet about shoulder width apart, the knees only slightly bent and the arms exceedingly loose. It was a stance made famous by Bruce Lee, but generally misunderstood by all those who imitated him, because it was not only a physical position; it was also a state of mind. It was an absence of force, a nothingness. Then for three or four seconds he simply waited—letting his energy subside while consciously creating a vacuum to draw the boy in. And when the boy finally took the bait, stepping in for another snap-kick, Lyons didn't exactly *make* the strike . . . he simply let it happen.

He struck with a loose right hand, turning it to a fist an instant before impact. He struck with only the hand, letting the body follow. Finally concentrating his energy at impact, he let it all explode.

The blow caught Hicks square in the mouth, held him for a stunned moment, then dropped him like a rag. When he finally managed to rise again, Lyons caught him a second time with a rising-kick to the groin. Then for at least another three or four minutes, the boy simply lay on his side spitting blood and traces of vomit.

"Lesson number one," Lyons said when the corporal had finally managed to crawl off the mat. "Never assume that you know more than your opponent. Learn to read him. Learn to assess his skills and probe his weak points. And then only after you have determined those weak points . . . only then do you make your move. Understood?"

Following another three more bouts of hand-to-hand, Lyons called for volunteers to attack him with knives. In response two stocky Latins rose to their feet. Once again, Lyons left them slumped on the mat.

"Lesson number two," Lyons said when his last two opponents had limped back to the ranks. "Just because you're armed, do not assume that you have an advantage."

Finally Lyons faced a dark and wiry private named Lasky, who was armed with an unloaded Uzi.

"Now, obviously when dealing with a problem like this," Lyons began, "you're going to have to be a little inventive. I mean you try to make a move on a man with a fully automatic weapon and you could find yourself in a pretty tight spot. For example, if I were to try to step in on this man from here, he'd probably blow me away before I could blink." He turned to the private with an easy grin. "What do you say, Private? Am I right?"

The private returned the grin with a nod, but did not lower the Uzi. "Yes, sir, you are definitely right. I would definitely blow you away at this distance, sir."

Lyons faced his audience again, and took another three or four paces closer to the private. "Even from this distance," he said, "I'd still be taking one hell of a chance. Right, Private?"

The private nodded again. "Yes, sir."

"But assuming I could get in here," Lyons continued, moving still a little closer to the private. "If I could get right in real tight like this, then maybe, just maybe..."

And suddenly lashing out with a quick right hand to grab the barrel of the Uzi, he struck with an open palm.

"Then I'd probably have a pretty good chance of taking this man out," he added with another grin.

Lyons wrenched the weapon away, and the man fell like a deadweight as Lyons struck him in the gut. In all the boy remained unmoving on the mat for at least thirty seconds while the others looked on in silence.

"Lesson number three," Lyons smiled, "there are no rules. Period."

"IMPRESSIVE," Stack said when the men had been dismissed. "Most impressive."

It was forty-five minutes after the hour. Although the injured had been sent to the medical station, traces of blood and vomit still remained on the mat. There were also a few hard glares from those who continued to linger by the fence.

"So what else can you teach us?" Stack asked with a tight smile.

Lyons accepted a towel from Schwarz and wiped the sweat from his face. "What else do you want to know, Colonel?"

"How about a little close quarter scramble with small arms?"

Lyons shrugged, then glanced quickly at Blancanales. "What about it, Pol? Do we do close quarter work with small arms?"

Blancanales eased himself off the low wall that ringed the quadrangle and slowly crossed the mat. "Night or day?" he asked.

"Night," Stack replied. "Definitely night."

"What kind of odds?"

Stack shook his head. "I don't know. How would four to one suit you?"

Blancanales ran a hand across his mouth and gazed out across the wall to the outline of what he supposed was a combat course. In addition to what looked like a fiberboard mock-up of tenements and factories, there was also something that resembled a schoolhouse.

"Four to one, huh?" Blancanales finally breathed. "Yeah, well I think we might able to show you a few new tricks at four to one."

"Fine," Stack replied. "Then I'll see you boys at nineteen-hundred hours. In the meantime, I suggest you get some rest, because I got a feeling you're going to need all your energy."

UPON RETURNING to their quarters, Schwarz insisted on conducting another quick search for concealed microphones. Blancanales remained fixed at the window, while Lyons showered and changed.

"So what do you think of it all?" Schwarz asked as he sagged back down onto his cot.

Lyons shook his head, reaching for a fresh pair of sweats. "I think we need to find out a whole lot more about what's going on around here," he said.

"How do you intend to do that?" Blancanales asked, still fixed at the window.

"Casually," Lyons smiled, "very casually."

Ten minutes later, dressed in gray sweats and running shoes, Lyons moved along a narrow track that skirted the edge of the quadrangle. He moved at a slow jog, seemingly intent on his rhythm, but occasionally nodding at passing personnel. As he neared the end of the quadrangle and approached a low rank of huts within a chain link enclosure, he heard a harsh voice shouting from the motor pool.

"You are entering a restricted area, sir! I repeat, that is a restricted area!"

Lifting a hand in acknowledgment, Lyons then slowly turned in a wide arc and headed back toward the track....

But not before he caught a quick glimpse of Molly Meekin, peering from that tiny aperture between the bricks of her cell.

9

The Wolf's Tooth unit, like all Special Forces operations, had originally been formed in response to unconventional, unpredictable and entirely ruthless acts of terrorism. To some extent, these acts were best exemplified by the 1983 bombing of the Marine Battalion Landing Team headquarters in Beirut—yellow Mercedes truck, packed with explosives, slammed into the Marine barracks and left 241 dead in the space of a few seconds.

In order to cope with this new kind of threat, the Special Forces Operations Detachments were subjected to a new kind of training regimen. They were expected to achieve expert proficiency with more than eighty light and heavy foreign weapons. They were expected to master at least one foreign language and to maintain their bodies in superb physical condition at all times. They were also expected to master the sort of skills that one would require to successfully score on the Wolf's Tooth combat course.

The combat course lay on the far eastern edge of the Wolf's Tooth compound. From a distance and through the dusk, it looked like a typical small village from anywhere in the world. On closer inspection, however, the features grew distinctly American. There was a fiberboard church, with the classic New England steeple. There was a mock-up of a colonial-style town house and a two-story saltbox, reminiscent of a West Virginian suburb. Finally there was even the front of a McDonald's replete with the golden arches.

"This then, gentlemen, is the field," said Colonel Stack. "This is the area you will either control or die in. There are no other alternatives."

It was a cool evening, with another chill desert wind blowing across the mesa. In anticipation of the chill, Able Team wore black Gor-Tex jerseys, black knit caps and knit gloves. Their opponents, charged with representing a regular Special Operations Force, were clad in drab green fatigues.

"So basically we're the bad guys, is that it?" Blancanales asked.

Stack smiled. "I guess that depends upon your viewpoint. The basic scenario is this: you gentlemen have just conducted a terrorist assault on this piece of the USA. In response, I have launched twelve members of my Domestic Insurrection team to hunt you down. Their weapons are identical to yours, but they will enjoy a slightly superior knowledge of the terrain. They will not, however, enjoy suicide options or the options of wholesale civilian slaughter."

Immediately following this explanation, Stack ordered Corporal Harris to distribute the weapons: fully automatic Nelspot paint ballers, with eighteen-load capabilities. Although the paint ball pellet was not exactly an accurate simulation of real weapon capabilities, Stack claimed he found it more realistic than the laser systems at close quarters. It was also cheaper. As a final point of instruction, Stack explained that prisoners would not be taken, and any shot between the head and groin was to be counted as fatal. Then came the brisk handshake, the curt nod and Able Team was left to their own devices.

TWO DARKENED LANES led from the wrought iron gates that formed the start of the combat course. At sixty-five yards the lanes converged into what was supposed to have been a village square. There were ranks of fabricated storefronts, a warehouse and a fire station. There were also dwellings above the shops and what might have been a beauty salon. Here and there mannequins had been placed on the street to represent civilians, but there were no real indications of life.

Lyons spent exactly nine minutes working out a strategy to meet Stack's team. In the main this strategy was based upon a single maxim: do the unexpected. Rather than waiting out the attack in one of the fabricated storefronts, Lyons led his men out of the square into the farthest recesses of the course: a narrow lane of fiberboard apartments that ultimately led to a chain link fence and out of the course grounds entirely.

"Look at it this way," Lyons told Schwarz and Blancanales, "we're playing their game on their ground. So if we're going to take them, we're going to have to play it like they've never seen it played before."

They were standing on a relatively open stretch of land that had been planted with shrubbery and eucalyptus trees to simulate a community playground. But already Lyons had begun to scan the far ground, the remote edges of the combat course.

"Are you thinking what I'm thinking?" Blancanales asked, also shifting his gaze to the chain link fence and storage sheds that marked the boundary of the course.

"It's kind of like this," Lyons replied. "Stack said his boys have a superior knowledge of the terrain, right? Well, okay, then let's see if we can't reverse that edge. Instead of meeting here or in that little village, we'll hit them from outside the course. We'll hit them from the storage sheds and the drainage ditch, then maybe even double back and take one of the referee towers. We will not engage them from fantasy land."

"I like it," Schwarz smiled. "I like it a whole lot."

"Well, that's good," Lyons smiled back, "because while you boys are kicking their butts, I think I might just use the time to take a little stroll somewhat farther afield . . . if you know what I'm saying."

THE FIRST CONTINGENT of Stack's team came at exactly nine o'clock. Schwarz had slipped onto the roof of a storage shed, while Blancanales had dropped into a drainage ditch. By way of a little diversion, Schwarz had set two mannequins in the window of a plywood warehouse and a third among the hedgerows. He had also strung trip-wires in the doorway of the schoolhouse and the entrance of an adjacent alley. Yet what initially alerted Schwarz and Blancanales were the footsteps; three, possibly four pairs of cautious footsteps moving along the deeper shadows of the lane.

"You hear that?" Schwarz whispered from his darkened recess above the storage shed.

"Yeah," Blancanales breathed. "I hear it."

"So how you want to play?"

Blancanales released the safety on his paint baller and gently eased the pistol into a firing position. "Let's just let them come right in," he smiled. "Let's just let them come right into Papa's arms."

It took another eighteen minutes for the Wolf's Team contingent to determine that their opponents were not waiting within one of the plywood apartments. The men had undoubtedly walked this lane a dozen times in simulated combat situations, yet they clearly began to grow uneasy. They were probably infuriated that their opponent had left the agreed upon confines of the course.

The team leader, a lanky corporal named Guitarez, motioned his two privates into the shadows of a hardware store. Then, apparently uncomfortable with the silence, he urged them into the shadows of the hedgerows. Finally, catching sight of the mannequins watching from the darkened window, Guitarez ordered a quick assault....

At which point Blancanales leveled his pistol and took the first man out with a shot between the shoulder blades.

"Shit!" the private moaned as the pellet exploded with a six-inch stain of red ink.

"Where the hell did that come from?" asked the bulky private beside him.

"Right here," Blancanales whispered as he squeezed off a second pellet that splattered directly over the man's heart.

Corporal Guitarez, with more than three hundred simulated combat hours under his belt, managed to survive exactly seven minutes longer than the others. Having apparently determined that Blancanales had fired from the drainage ditch, he attempted to circle around the park and skirt the edge of the chain link fence. In another time and place it might have worked. However, his path took him directly into Schwarz's line of fire.

"Looking for someone?" Schwarz asked softly, still not revealing himself.

"What the—"

The inked pellet exploded in a lovely burst of crimson directly between the Corporal's eyes.

"Guess what?" Schwarz whispered. "You're dead."

TWO HUNDRED YARDS from the chain link fence, Carl Lyons also whispered in the dark. He whispered to himself, not really thinking, just simply venting a little frustration. What the hell is going on in this place? he wondered. Despite the chill of the desert wind, his clothing was drenched with perspiration. He had also cut his hand slipping through the razor wire and had probably bruised the ball of his left foot leaping from the fence.

But despite these minor discomforts and the somewhat greater risk of discovery, he was genuinely glad to be playing another kind of game with Colonel Stack's Domestic Counterinsurrection Force.

From where he squatted in the deeper shadows beyond the motor pool, he could see two structures that intrigued him. The first looked like some sort of concrete bunker but may have also served as a communications tank. The second, unless he was badly mistaken by the shadows, looked exactly like a miniature mock-up of the White House.

Lyons waited . . . watching, listening, consciously steadying himself against the chill of the desert wind. Then slowly rising to the balls of his feet again, he slid onto a narrow ledge above some sort of command post. As far as he could tell, the miniature White House was actually part of a much larger model that included a key stretch of Pennsylvania Avenue, the Washington Monument and Capitol Hill. There was also a somewhat less detailed model of the Congressional offices, Lincoln Memorial and the Department of Justice. Apparently constructed of plywood and fiberglass, the models had been laid out on some sort of circular grid. There were even plastic elms along the Reflecting Pool, and tiny plastic automobiles along the highway. But what ultimately left Lyons motionless, straining in blackness for some shred of understanding, were the tanks—more than a dozen scale model plastic tanks, fixed in a converging line across the Potomac.

In all Lyons must have spent the better part of twenty minutes crouched in the darkness, staring at the model of his nation's capital. Twice he heard the echo of slow footsteps from the motor pool and what may have been voices from the sheds. He vaguely wished he had brought a camera, one of those infrared jobs. He also wished he was armed with something more than a compressed air pellet gun.

BLANCANALES WITHDREW another plastic tube of ink pellets and inserted them into the chamber. Although he liked the weight of the gun, he wished he was packing something larger than a paint baller.

"So?" he whispered, scanning the empty lane beyond the drainage ditch. "So?"

Schwarz shrugged, also scanning the lane. "So let's just do it. Know what I mean? Let's just do it."

From the drainage ditch they moved past a fiberboard mock-up of a suburban police station and another row of modest dwellings. There was even a mailbox on the corner and two telephone poles. In line with their original strategy, however, Schwarz and Blancanales worked the fringe of this illusionary world. They moved along the cart paths behind false fronts. They kept to the catwalk just inside the course perimeter. Then finally slipping into another storage shed, they once more paused in the darkness.

"So?" Blancanales asked, hunkering down among a mess of electrical wires, circuit breakers and what felt like the base of an arc light.

"So maybe we've just stumbled onto something," Schwarz replied as his fingers explored what felt like an industrial light bulb.

Although they had earlier heard voices and more footsteps from the village square, it was once again very quiet.

"Ever been on a movie set?" Schwarz asked, his fingers now exploring what felt like a mobile spotlight.

"Yeah, what about it?"

"From in front of the camera, everything looks completely real. Take a few steps in back of the camera and it's another story."

"So?"

"So, we just walked behind the camera."

His fingers inching in the blackness, Schwarz finally disentangled the spotlight from the coils of dusty wire. There were also boxes of government issue flashlights and even a bullhorn.

"It's just like Lyons said," Schwarz continued as he blindly began feeling for switches and batteries. "Out there we've got a bunch of kids playing hide-and-seek in make-believe land. In here you and I are playing anything-goes. Now, I'm not saying those guys aren't good. But basically they're still a bunch of kids, and all we've got to do to spoil their game is pull the plug on their fantasy. Get what I'm saying?"

Although Schwarz couldn't actually see Blancanales's face through the blackness, he could certainly sense the grin.

"Yeah," Blancanales whispered. "I think I know exactly what you're saying."

LYONS WAS STILL CROUCHED in the darkness. Having finally moved past the miniaturized model of the capital, he now paused again in the shadows. As far as he could tell, he had entered some sort of storage area. All around him stood heaps of packing crates, stacked lumber and entrenching equipment. There were also two jeeps fitted with twin 50-caliber machine guns and an inflatable landing craft. There was one object that fixed his attention: a blue Honda Civic, with bullet holes in the right front fender and a smashed windshield.

He inched a little closer, slipping into the flapping shadows of a canvas tent. He waited until the footsteps of a guard receded, then silently moved into the shadows of another packing crate. Finally, dropping to his belly, he crawled across the cold pavement until he reached deflated tires.

He paused again...waiting, listening, straining in the darkness for voices from across the compound. He rolled onto his back and inched up to the driver's door. Then pausing again for another forty seconds, he finally slid a hand inside the shattered window and eased the door open.

There was the odor of gasoline inside and fragments of glass on the floor. There were also traces of what might have been dried blood on the dashboard and long strands of matted hair. But what finally confirmed Lyons's hunch was what he found beneath the driver's seat: a speeding ticket issued to one Miss Molly Meekin of Albuquerque.

CORPORAL ANDREW SHAFT'S suspicions were confirmed by the traces of mud on the chain link fence: six distinct traces of mud indicating that his quarry had definitely scaled the fence and were now waiting in one of the storage facilities. Although the corporal had not been particularly impressed by what he had thus far seen of Able Team's performance, he had to admit that their current strategy was pretty clever: keep to the perimeters, keep to the ground that was not officially part of the combat course and keep your enemy guessing. Smart. Real smart.

He scrambled back into the shadows of a plaster oak where his six-man team was waiting. Occasionally erratic in the slack time, these men could not have been tighter under pressure. And although these night games did not exactly constitute real pressure, he could feel the tension amongst the group.

"What do you say?" Crabb, a quirky veteran of the Grenada invasion, asked.

"I say we're looking good," Shaft replied. "I say we're looking real good."

"So you got 'em pegged?" asked a lean ex-Ranger named Hodges.

"Soon enough," Shaft smiled. "Soon enough."

They moved out in a staggered line with Shaft on the point and Hodges taking up the rear. In addition to their paint ballers, Shaft had packed an AN-PVS-4 Starlite system with a 20 mm second generation intensifier. He had also packed a couple of M-18 smoke grenades and three canisters of antiriot tear gas...in clear violation of combat course rules.

He brought his team to a halt beside the first row of sheds, then switched on the Starlite scope and scanned the blackness beyond.

"Anything?" an eighteen-month veteran of the Nicaraguan action whispered.

Shaft slowly eased the scope to the left until the intensified circle of light fell upon the last shed. "Maybe," he breathed. Then focusing on a broken padlock and another trace of mud on the pavement, "Maybe."

"So how do we proceed?" another veteran of Special Forces action in the Central American jungles asked.

Shaft switched off the Starlite scope and returned it to his Alice Pack. "Well, I'll tell you," he drawled softly. "The way I see it we got two choices. We can either play it by the book and hit them head-on or we can bend a few rules."

"What you talking about?" Hodges whispered.

"I'm talking about this," Shaft smiled...and withdrew the canister of tear gas. "I'm talking about this baby right here."

They moved out in another staggered line. Once again Shaft took the point while Hodges brought up the rear. Although Crabb may have sensed that something was not right after only twenty yards, it was not until they had reached the first shed that he actually said anything.

"Hey," he whispered to Shaft. "You feel that?"

Shaft did not even bother turning around. "Feel what?"

"That."

Shaft paused, glanced back over his shoulder. "What are you talking about, man?"

"I'm talking about that."

"About what?"

But it wasn't until Crabb actually heard the double click of a cocking pistol that he could even begin to articulate his fears.

And by that time, Blancanales had already hit them with the blinding spotlight while Schwarz's voice boomed through the bullhorn: "You men are in our line! Throw down your weapons and place your hands on your heads!"

"Holy shit!" Hodges shouted as he tried to scurry from the light. "Holy shit!"

Crabb, too, was shouting out obscenities as that blinding light burst in his eyes. But it wasn't until the pellets started flying that Corporal Shaft began to lose his cool, screaming, "Do something! Do something!"

By this point there was really nothing left to do but wince with the sting of bursting pellets.

It was Blancanales who actually fired first, squeezing off four pellets from behind the blinding spotlight. His first shot may have been a little wide, his second, third and fourth were dead on, catching two men in the gut and another in the ribs. Then as Crabb and Hodges attempted to slip back into the shadows of a plaster elm, Schwarz also squeezed off a couple of pellets—one to Crabb's back, another into Hodges's chest.

The fifth to catch a splattering pellet was one of the Grenada veterans, a prematurely balding private named Cole.

Although he, too, had been momentarily disoriented by the blinding spotlight and booming voice, he had finally managed to at least squeeze off one shot in defence—a remarkably calm and collected shot at what appeared to be Schwarz's head. The "head," however, was actually just the outline of the bullhorn, and Schwarz's return fire caught him directly between the eyes.

Which finally left only Shaft.

"You useless idiots!" Shaft began screaming, as he turned to face his ink-splattered team. "What the hell do you think you're doing!"

Under the circumstances, it was not an entirely unwarranted question...although technically dead the soldiers still saw fit to level their pistols and riddle Shaft's buttocks with pellets.

THREE HUNDRED YARDS NORTHEAST from the rest of the group, Carl Lyons was also playing a little game of hide-and-seek...but on a somewhat more serious level.

It was particularly cold here, with nothing to keep that chill wind racing across the empty flatland and numbing every inch of exposed skin. He also found the stench of creosote a little offensive and his bruised foot was beginning to slow him down. But it was the guards that concerned him the most at this point.

There were two of them—two obviously half-frozen privates watching from a tower at the end of the paved road. Although there were also spotlights on the tower, they relied on a Starlite scope to scan the ground. And to make matters worse, they were armed with weapons far more lethal than air-powered pellet guns.

In all Lyons spent about seven minutes weighing the odds, trying to calculate his chances of reaching the Quonset huts that lay beyond the shadow of that tower. He tried to calculate if it was worth it . . . if it was worth the risk of blowing everything for one or two whispered words with the girl he assumed was Molly Meekin.

Severson had told them not to make it a priority. He didn't even know if her disappearance was connected to events at the Wolf's Tooth compound.

Lyons hesitated before crossing the eighty yards of exposed ground, taking one last moment to weigh the odds against the unlikely rewards. Then glancing up once more to the tower, he moved out.

He moved at another half crouch, keeping to the shadows of what may have been a recreation room. Despite the cold, he was sweating again and he was thankful for the wind that covered the sound of his footsteps on the gravel.

He paused at the end of the brickwork, once more peering out to the tower. It seemed to rise out of the chaparral like the skeleton of some prehistoric beast. The guards also looked a little inhuman, hunched against the biting wind, scanning the landscape with what might have been an elongated eye. Then taking a deep breath and consciously willing the guards to look away, he sprinted across the last thirty yards.

He hesitated for at least another four minutes after finally reaching the Quonset hut where he had caught a glimpse of the girl. Quite apart from the risk of getting caught, it had crossed his mind that there was a degree of liability in merely communicating with her. After all, there was no telling what her emotional status was at this point—whether she had turned or even broken. In the end, however, he decided that it was a chance he had to take. For reasons that he couldn't exactly name, he simply had to let her know that she wasn't alone any longer.

It took him exactly three minutes to pick the lock, another eighteen seconds to silently ease back the door and slip into blackness. Then for at least another fifteen seconds, he simply stood there . . . listening to the sound of her terrified breath.

"Don't turn on the light, Miss Meekin."

"Who are you?"

"A friend."

"But how did—"

"Never mind how. Just listen for a moment. Are you being held here against your will?"

"Yes, but—"

"Do you know why?"

He could still only make out her dim outline, and he was certain that she was crying, silently sobbing and shaking her head.

"Because I saw what they did to that soldier . . . because I saw it."

"Saw what, Molly? Saw them do what?"

Then although he still couldn't see her, the flood of tears was obvious.

"Saw them murder him! Saw them murder him with machine guns simply because he was trying to make a phone call."

He left her crying in the darkness. Even though he had assured her that he would eventually get her out, she still couldn't seem to stop crying.

COLONEL STACK was furious. Able Team had tagged ten of his fourteen men, and had not suffered a single hit . . . *Not one!*

He shut his eyes, consciously willing his anger to subside before turning to face Corporal Harris and his two "surviving" privates in the village square. His presence on the course constituted yet another infraction of the rules. He didn't give a damn. He wasn't concerned that he had supplied his men with infrascopes and a Nytech image intensifier. He cared only of winning.

"Which is why you men are going to start kicking some ass. Is that clear?"

Corporal Harris responded with a stony nod and a quick glance to the privates beside him. "Perfectly, sir."

"And just to ensure that you do not totally blow this round, too, I'm going to make it real easy for you." He pointed to the roof of a town house mock-up. "You see that man up there?"

Harris responded with another nod, while the two lean privates remained silent. "Yes, sir."

"That man is your spotter. There are four others like him on adjacent roofs. They are going to direct you to the enemy by means of this microphone. You are to conceal this microphone on your person and you are to follow the commands to the letter. Is that clear?"

"Yes, sir."

"Now, if you have any misgivings about the so-called ethical implications of these tactics, I suggest you take the matter up with your chaplain at a later date. Because right now I just want to see an effective performance. Is that clear?"

"Yes, sir."

"Then why the hell are you standing?"

"Because, Sir . . ."

"Because what, soldier?"

"Because I didn't give him permission to leave," Lyons said behind them as he squeezed off three more perfectly placed pellets.

ALTHOUGH STACK OFFERED Lyons nothing beyond a stiff handshake and a mumbled "congratulations," Corporal Harris turned out to be a better sportsman. It was now almost two o'clock in the morning. The wind had died and the moon had finally risen above the chaparral.

"I've got to admit it," Harris said as he handed Lyons a cup of steaming coffee, "you guys definitely know how to move."

Lyons accepted the cup with a friendly nod. "Well, thank you, Corporal."

"In fact, you probably set some kind of course record here tonight . . . what with the odds and all."

"Well, we didn't do anything we can't teach you how to do for yourself."

"Yeah, well that's the point. Maybe you guys should think about coming on board as something more than just instructors."

Lyons glanced over to Stack, who was softly conferring with one of the privates Blancanales had pasted by the storage sheds.

"Oh, I wouldn't worry about him," Harris smiled. "He just doesn't like losing. But you give him a couple of days to think about what happened here tonight, and he'll be asking you to come aboard himself."

"As what?" Lyons asked, now stealing a glance at the dim outline of Quonset huts where he had met the girl.

"You name it," Harris replied. "Special weapons and tactics, rapid deployment teams, unconventional warfare—we got everything here. And just between us, let me tell you that the benefits are sweet, real sweet."

Lyons cocked his head with a small grin, shifting his gaze to the blackened landscape beyond the last fence. "Don't get me wrong." He finally sighed. "I appreciate what you're saying, but I think we might have a little trouble fitting in. I mean we might be able to deal with a guy like your colonel, but sooner or later we're going to end up taking orders from a bunch of flat-assed civilians, and that would definitely cause us problems."

Harris smiled, a long and slow smile that Lyons would think about for a long time after. "Yeah, well that's the whole point of the Wolf's Tooth," he said. "We're going to fix it so that there won't be no more civilian command—not ever."

10

Lyle Severson shifted his gaze above the mantle to meet the vaguely sad eyes of Thomas Jefferson. Although the portrait may not have been the most inspired reproduction Severson had ever seen, there was definitely something intriguing about the man's eyes—they seemed to reach across the centuries, comprehending everything that was happening today.

"I suppose we should probably talk about what we're going to do if our worst fears are realized," Severson said at last.

Harwood took another sip of brandy and shivered as he felt the draft from beneath the door. "Meaning?"

"Meaning that we should probably start talking about getting you out of the country."

It was just after three o'clock in the morning. The safehouse, a half-timbered cottage that may have once been a Virginia smokehouse, could not have been colder. The view through frosted windows was also pretty bleak: leafless oaks beside the frozen stream, a lonely road heaped with snow. There was, however, something oddly comforting about that portrait of Jefferson propped on the mantle, and an equally compassionate portrait of Lincoln beside it.

"Look, before we start running for cover," Harwood said, "maybe we'd better take it from the top again."

He had slept no more than six or seven hours since arriving at this cottage two days earlier. He wasn't actually tired—exhausted maybe, but not really tired.

"All right," Severson sighed. "From the top then." He glanced at his wristwatch, a gold Rolex awarded to him after twenty-one years of service in America's secret wars. "Exactly thirteen hours ago, I met with an old friend from the Naval Special Warfare group."

Harwood started to ask a question, but Severson silenced him with a hand. "You don't need to know his name, John. All you need to know is that the guy is trustworthy."

"Is he willing to go on the record?"

"Not yet."

"Then what's the point?"

"The point is that he says it's real—that there is definitely a faction within this nation's military that has gone way out of control."

"And by way out of control, you mean exactly what?"

"I mean that they're probably planning to take over the government," he sighed. "I mean that they're actively planning to turn this country into a military dictatorship."

Harwood let his head slump to the back of his chair: a bentwood rocker that must have been at least a hundred years old. The other furniture around him—the flowered settee, the chintz sofa, the oil lamp and occasional table—were also from a seemingly simpler and more secure era.

"But how?" he finally whispered. "How could something like this happen?"

Severson shrugged. "I suppose in one sense it's simply a consequence of the Special Forces mentality. Take the Naval Special Warfare group, for example. Like the other Special Forces groups, it was originally set up to fight a different kind of war: fast and dirty. In addition to the SEAL teams, they've got a light attack helo squadron, a Special

Boat Squadron and a couple of Special Warfare units. But the main difference between the Naval Special Warfare group and the regular navy is their independence. To put it bluntly, they're basically a power unto themselves. We can't cut their budget, because they're funded directly through the Pentagon. We can't cut their command line, because the channels are autonomous.''

Harwood shut his eyes as if to absorb the full weight of Severson's analysis. ''What about . . . what's his name? Jim Lindsey?'' he finally asked.

Severson shook his head. ''Lindsey may be the official Special Forces commander, but we're no longer dealing with an official link. We're dealing with a secret link, probably set up by Rambling Ray Doyle and his cronies at the Pentagon.''

''And how far do these links extend?''

Severson shook his head again. ''I don't know, but I think we now have to assume that the whole infrastructure may be dirty, that the Special Forces are only the advance team and that if they're successful the whole military may take part.''

Harwood pressed a pale hand to his eyes and took a long, slow breath. ''So how the hell do we fight them? If the whole damn military is in on it, how the hell do we fight them?''

Severson shifted his gaze back to that portrait of Jefferson. ''With everything we've got,'' he said softly. ''We fight them with everything we've got.''

They parted in a foyer that smelled of leaf mold and a century of wood smoke. In addition to a portrait of Washington, there were also two little drypoints of the second Continental Congress and an old etching of Benjamin Franklin. What had always fascinated Severson, however, was the musket tacked to the wall above the door—a rusted and worm-eaten thing that probably hadn't been fired in at least two hundred years.

"By the way," Severson said from the doorway. "It looks like Lyons found the Meekin girl."

Harwood had also been staring at that musket. "Alive?"

"For the moment."

"What do you mean?"

"I mean that apparently she was a witness to Gibb's murder, so I don't imagine they plan to keep her around indefinitely."

"So what are we going to do about it?"

Severson started to shake his head again, but suddenly stopped. "Don't worry," he finally smiled. "Carl Lyons isn't the kind of guy that would just leave a nineteen-year-old girl sitting around waiting to take a bullet in the head. I mean, that's just not his style."

11

Lyons curled his fingers around the chain link and gazed out to the wastes beyond. Although there were pines and traces of snow along the mesa's rim, it still seemed a foreboding place...a place of dry roads and cracked earth, flat horizons and sterile thunder.

"So?" Blancanales said after joining Lyons at the fence.

"So, what the hell," Lyons whispered. "Let's just go for it. Let's just wait until dark, and then go for it."

It was the afternoon of the fourth day. Having spent the morning lecturing to seventy-five men on the SERE course —survival, evasion, resistance and escape—his throat was as dry as the dust at his feet. He had further bruised his knuckles on the jaw of a private from Alabama, and he was tired, bone tired. However, he saw no other alternative but to go for it...to wait until dark, and then go for it.

"Why don't you run through it again?" he said, turning to Blancanales.

Pol shrugged, as he kicked his toe in the dust. "According to this guy called Cookie, the really critical stuff went down last spring. April, May, something like that."

"Yeah, but who's Cookie?" Schwarz asked. "How do we know he was telling you the truth?"

"Cook, Alfred E. Believe it or not, I knew him in Nam, then bumped into him later in Laos. He may not be the nicest guy in the world, but I don't think he had any reason to lie.''

"So, what's his story?"

Blancanales shrugged again. "No story really. I was having a beer in the officers' canteen last night and he just walks up to me and starts talking about old times. Says that he was wondering when I'd show up at this place, because all the old jungle rats are here. I ask him what's going on and then he starts telling me about the April games.''

"How long did he say he's been here?" Schwarz asked.

"Ten months, give or take. Got himself posted here from Delta One as a patrol leader, then moved into tactical planning after some lieutenant bought it in Beirut.''

"And he's reliable?" Lyons asked.

Blancanales shrugged again. "Well, considering the fact that he's a total animal, yeah.''

"So what did he say about the April games?" Schwarz asked.

"He said they were weird," Blancanales answered. "He said that supposedly the scenario called for a defensive posture. Bunch of terrorist-backed insurgents take over the White House and the Senate, right? So his team is supposed to move in and take it back. But that's not the way they played it. They played it from a completely offensive posture. White House and Senate are conducting business as usual, and his team moves in and wipes them out—no terrorists, no insurgents, just a pure and simple hit.''

Schwarz and Lyons exchanged a quick glance, then Lyons returned his gaze to the flat horizon. Trucks, or possibly tanks, were throwing up trails of dust in the distance, but otherwise there were no sounds and no movement apart from the wind.

"We're going to need proof," Lyons said at last. "We can't just take that guy's word for it.''

"Yeah, well that's the whole point," Blancanales replied. "It's all on record. Every move of every game is written down for later analysis."

"And the records are kept where? Stack's office?"

Blancanales nodded. "According to Cookie, yeah. Records of the games are kept in Stack's office."

"We also have a probable confirmation of that from Harwood," Schwarz added. "Everything's in what they call the Strat Room, which is directly attached to Stack's office."

"But it's got to be under lock and key, right?" Lyons said.

Schwarz shrugged. "Depends how you define a lock. Frankly I don't think we're going to have much of a problem getting our hands on the stuff. I think the problem will come later...trying to get out of here."

Lyons gradually shifted his gaze to the south and the long road between those dung-colored hills. "What about the armory?"

Blancanales followed Lyons's gaze. "Weapons of choice around are Heckler and Koch MP-5s and French MAT-49s. Sniper's tend to use the M-21 systems, which includes a variable power sight."

"What about the heavier stuff?"

"Well, if they come after us in choppers we can always try to hit them with a shoulder-launch, but you got to bear in mind that those choppers are pretty sophisticated. I mean they've even got a couple of the new Nighthawks out here, fitted with Cyclops systems and holographic image projectors."

"And for fast ground pursuit?"

"For fast pursuit they seem to be a little thin. All I've seen are jeeps with mounted quad fifty's, and these weird Italian jobs called Gorgonas, which are kind of like fighting family vans."

"So, what kind of timing are we talking about?"

"The timing's going to have to be tight," Schwarz replied. "Twenty minutes after I hit Stack's office, we had better be in a vehicle and on the road."

"Which means getting to the motor pool by 2100," Blancanales added, "grabbing one of those quad fifty jeeps and not slowing down for anything or anyone."

"Except the Meekin girl," Lyons said softly. Then in response to Schwarz's questioning look, "Well, you don't expect to just leave her here, do you? Well, do you?"

"NO," MOLLY whispered to herself. "He won't just leave me here."

It was cold in her cell. Even with the space heater turned on full, it was still very cold. At one point during the night, after waking in a shivering chill, she decided that she must have come down with a fever. But then climbing onto the table and easing herself up to the small opening, she had finally seen the distant snow along that flat horizon.

And somehow that vision of snow, like the memory of a man whispering in the dark, had filled her with lingering hope.

For a long time after Lyons had come to her cell, she had been able to think of little else. Although she knew nothing about him, not even what he looked like, she was certain that he hadn't been lying when he told her he'd be back to get her out. It hadn't been just a trick to get her to talk. It hadn't been just a dream.

She shut her eyes, clutching the blanket a little tighter to her shoulders and trying to recapture the memory of him standing in the doorway. In the beginning, whenever she thought about him, she could only recall the sound of his voice—the soft, but assured way he had pronounced her name. She tried not to think about him too often for fear of wearing the memory thin. Then three days ago, waking at dawn to the throb of distant choppers, she had suddenly recalled a vision of his outline in the blackness—a tall and lean shadow, whispering, "Don't turn on the light."

12

It was half past eight in the evening when Gadgets Schwarz set out across the compound en route to Colonel Stack's office. He was clothed once more in black—black Gore-Tex, black Reeboks and black field trousers. In addition to his cat burglar's kit, containing an assortment of looped wires, dental picks and a battery powered drill, he also carried his .45 auto and an H&K MP-5 with a NATO specification load. He had also packed a standard fragmentation grenade, but at the last minute Lyons had made him leave it behind, claiming that it was inconsistent with the cover.

"Think of it as another training exercise," Lyons had said. "They brought us in to show them a few new wrinkles, so tonight we're going to be testing their security system."

"And if they start shooting?" Schwarz asked.

"Then it's no longer a training exercise."

Stack's office lay on the western rim of the compound, a simple brick building, adjacent to the briefing room and living quarters. The whitewashed flagstones had been laid between a meager cactus garden. A little shade was provided by the Joshua trees. Beyond the garden lay a second brick complex housing the communications center and finally the security towers.

Schwarz spent about fifteen minutes working out his approach to Stack's office. Although he had spent the afternoon reviewing a crude map of the grounds, there was no substitute for an on-site inspection. So he waited...crouched in the shadows of a radio shack, noting the lay of the shadows and the sound of the wind through the nest of antennae. Then glancing up once more at the hulking tower, he moved off across the gravel.

"If you're challenged," Lyons had said, "just play it cool. Give them five points for being on their toes, but give them hell for not having spotted you sooner."

"What if they don't buy it?"

"Then kick them in the teeth."

He paused again where the shadows of the tower met the shadows of those Joshua trees. While he couldn't actually see the guards in the tower, it was easy enough to imagine them. They'd be sipping black coffee, chatting about women they had probably never known, scanning the perimeter through a night-vision system and fingering M-14 National Match rifles with variable power sights. He glanced again to the tower before running the last twenty yards to the door.

"The locks are a joke," Lyons had said. "A standard Medeco on the door, a drop latch on the windows. Inside, however, it's a different matter. Inside, you've got a strike system."

He went for the Medeco, because he could work unseen in the shadows and because he was familiar with the action. He used the looped wire to work the spring bolt, then a second bit of wire to work the cylinder. In all it took him roughly four minutes to open the door, then another three minutes for his eyes to become sufficiently adjusted to the darkness.

There were few personal touches in Stack's office: a photograph of the man amid Saigon rubble, another of him smiling from the steps of the Fort Bragg briefing room, a third and fourth taken from the edge of a landing strip in some Central American jungle. There were also the obligatory commendations on the walls and a silver plated .45 in a glass case.

Three filing drawers lined the far wall, with steel cabinet locks that virtually begged to be cracked. But there was also a Sonitrol high apprehension alarm system, probably tied into the tower.

Schwarz dropped to his knees, withdrew a mini Mag-lite, and held it between his teeth. Then gently following the wires with his fingers until he found the trip, he turned his attention back to the locks. As he finally slid back the drawer, he couldn't help whispering a private prayer, *Please don't let there be ultrasonics.*

He waited another two or three minutes, shivering a little as a drop of perspiration inched along his spine. The colonel's files were arranged alphabetically—the critical entries were in chronological order: January, February, March and April.

"Obviously he's not going to keep the really heavy stuff in his office," Lyons had said. "Mission orders, SOFCOM dispatches, J.C. cables—that material will be in the safes. Don't worry about it; we're just after the Game Reports."

The March and April "Capital Defense" Game Reports had been bound in buff folders and labeled according to their dates. There were two red SECRET stamps on the cover and another on the title page. The cover letter was addressed to the SOFCOM Fort Bragg, with copies to Rambling Ray Doyle and Arthur Matoon Clancy. Although the opening remarks were oddly informal, thereafter it was all business, with tactical summaries along the left margins and casualty estimates along the right.

Schwarz spent another three or four minutes leafing through the March and April Game Reports before finally slipping them under his Gore-Tex jersey. As he moved out again through the blackness, he was suddenly very conscious that he had passed the point of no return...that he was now in violation of federal espionage laws.

Schwarz was nine feet beyond the office door when he saw the guard. A bulky figure in winter dress, the man stood at the end of the flagstones. A discarded coffee cup and cigarette lay at his feet. What may have been a key chain dangled from his left hand. He finally turned his head to the left and squinted into the blackness...within seconds he held his M-16 in combat readiness.

Schwarz rose to his feet with an easy grin and approached the man slowly. He was careful to keep his hands visible and his posture casual. At fifteen feet he even nodded with a slight shrug and an exaggerated shiver as if to make a statement about the cold.

"How's it going, soldier?"

The boy returned the nod, but still didn't lower his weapon. He was a muscular youth, with cropped blond hair and what may have been a shrapnel scar along the jaw. Probably no older than twenty-four or twenty-five, his hard blue eyes had definitely seen action before.

"I think you'd better stay right where you are, sir."

Schwarz cocked his head with another easy grin. "Say it again, soldier?"

"Sir, if you could just stand where you are and put your hands on your head."

"Hands on my head? What are you talking about, soldier?"

"Sir, you are in a restricted area, and I've got orders to arrest anyone found here without the proper authority."

Then, although Schwarz didn't let the grin fade, he finally shook his head and stopped. "All right, soldier, you win. Security check complete and you pass with flying colors. Now, how about showing me where you got that coffee, because I happen to be freezing my ass off?''

Instead of returning the grin, however, the guard just kept looking at him. "I'm sorry, sir, but I'm going to have to take you in."

Schwarz slowly let his grin sag to a frustrated smirk. Then shaking his head with a hard sigh, he casually took another three steps forward. He also dropped his hands.

"Soldier, do you mind if I ask what your name is?"

"Lester, Private L. Now, if you would just turn around, sir, and put your—"

"Private Lester, how long have you been serving in this man's Army?"

"Five years, sir. Now as I was saying, if you would just turn around and—"

"Five years, huh? Well, let me tell you something, son. If you plan to last another five years in this man's Army there's something you had better learn. Before you go and arrest a man, even a man who happens to be the guest of your commanding officer, you had better be ready to blow him away at the first sign of resistance. Because if you hesitate, even for a fraction of a second, you could wind up in one hell of a lot of trouble. Now, do you follow what I'm saying, son?"

"Yes, sir, I do. But I'm afraid that I'm still going to have to ask that—"

"And are you entirely ready to pull that trigger at the first sign of resistance, soldier?"

"Yes, sir, I am."

"Well, somehow I don't believe you, soldier. Somehow I just don't believe you."

And in the awkward split second that followed, while the boy just kept staring at him, Schwarz struck.

He struck with a low kick to the boy's left knee, while simultaneously grabbing the barrel of the rifle. Then dropping his shoulder and bringing down his heel on the boy's instep, he struck again with an elbow to the jaw.

The boy crumpled with a low groan, sagging to his knees as his mouth filled with blood. When he vainly tried to pull his weapon free, Schwarz hit him again with a hardened palm to the bridge of the nose. But although the boy still wouldn't lie down and be quiet, Schwarz couldn't quite bring himself to hit him any more.

LYONS HAD ALSO been having second thoughts about inflicting bodily harm on American soldiers. After slipping past the assembly yard and another rank of Quonset huts, he and Blancanales eventually found their path blocked by two guards—two bored and tired guards posted just inside the motor pool. It was now just after nine o'clock. The immediate vicinity was silent and dark, but there was a fair amount of activity along the southern perimeter, where units from a Psyop Group were testing the radio links.

"It's your call," Blancanales whispered when they had drawn in sight of the guards. "You want me to take them out, I'll take them out. You want me to divert them, I'll divert them. I kind of have the feeling, however, that we're not going to get too far by just talking to them."

Lyons withdrew a nine-inch Trail Master—double edged, stainless steel. Like Schwarz he also carried an H&K MP-5 and a .45 auto on his hip.

"Tell me about them," he said softly. "How would they play it if we pissed them off?"

Blancanales took another long look at the outline of the guards, now apparently sipping coffee from a thermos. "They'd play it by the book," he finally said. "They'd ask us to surrender our weapons, then call the night watch."

"And if we gave them a hard time?"

"They'd do whatever was necessary to subdue us."

Lyons replaced the knife and withdrew his H&K. "But it's only for show," he said. "You understand what I'm saying? It's only for show."

They moved out in a full crouch, keeping to the edge of the path and testing each step before planting their feet. The moon had finally inched past the clouds, and the light was still thin between the surrounding huts. At thirty yards they paused again in the shadow of another storage shed. Then skirting the chain link fence that led to the gates, they slipped inside the motor pool.

They waited another thirty seconds in the shadows of the fuel pumps while Lyons calculated distances and Blancanales shed his gun. Then finally exchanging a last quick glance, they moved out again. At twenty yards Lyons slid off into the shadow of a junked transport while Blancanales rose to his feet and addressed the guards.

"Question," he said with an obviously drunken slur. "Where in hell is the nearest latrine?"

The guards responded with dull smiles. The taller of the two men was a beefy private named Simpson. The other was thin and dark—and although Blancanales couldn't recall his name, he was pretty certain that the man was Harold Gibb's killer.

"The latrine, sir," Simpson said, "is back the other way and to your left."

Blancanales glanced back over his shoulder, then shook his head. "Nope," he slurred. "Never make it. No way, no how."

The guards exchanged knowing glances, while Blancanales turned his eyes to a line of four jeeps parked beside the service bay.

"Okay, let me ask you something else," he drawled. "What would it take to convince you boys to let me borrow one of them vehicles?"

The guards exchanged another wary glance, but didn't seem to know quite what to say in response.

"So how about it?" Blancanales continued. "What would you boys say, if I borrowed one of them nice little vehicles of yours?"

Although Simpson continued to smile, the dark one had finally begun to finger his weapon. "Look, sir, you have got to move on now," he said. "You understand? You have got to move on right now."

But Blancanales simply continued staring at the jeeps. "Tell you what I'll do. You boys hand over the keys to one of them vehicles, and I'll take you out to a little place I know few miles from here. Now, how's that sound? Three of us pile into that there jeep and have ourselves a little party?"

"I'm afraid not, sir," said Simpson. "Now, if you would just move on out of this area . . ."

But by this time Lyons had already slid out of the darkness, released the safety on his H&K and leveled the muzzle at the thin guard's back.

"I'm afraid you boys just made a big mistake," he said softly. "Now instead of kicking back and sucking a beer, you're going to have to spend the night in that service bay."

IT TOOK EXACTLY seven minutes to handcuff the guards to the universal joint of an armored personnel carrier, gag them with oil rags and secure the door of the service bay. Although neither man offered any real resistance, the smoldering hatred could not have been more obvious. Outside in the yard, however, it had grown even colder, with the wind literally howling through the chain link fence.

"Pick us out a good one," Lyons breathed as Blancanales inspected the line of jeeps. "I got the feeling that we're going to need all the help we can get."

Blancanales lifted the hood to inspect the jeep, then slid behind a four-barreled assembly of 50-caliber machine guns mounted on a swivel to the rear of the jeep. "How about this one?" he asked, casually testing the action.

Lyons nodded. "That one looks fine."

It was 9:38 p.m. when Blancanales finally eased the jeep out of the motor pool. In addition to the extra drums of gasoline, he had also packed an extra three hundred rounds of 50-caliber ammunition. But ultimately it was a trade off, he had told Lyons. Load the jeep and you lose the speed. Strip her and you're defenseless.

Beyond the motor pool there were at least half a dozen loitering men on night watch. Only one or two of them, however, paid any attention to the cruising jeep and they were probably too cold to even care. Then came the relatively deserted stretch of road to the east end of the perimeter where Schwarz was hopefully waiting beside a laundry room with the Game Reports tucked under his arm.... And then there would be one final stop to make: at the Quonset huts where Molly Meekin was waiting.

THERE WERE THREE GUARDS in the tower overlooking the sector where Molly was imprisoned. From the edge of the path that led to her hut, Lyons could see them quite clearly: two apparently chatting inside the glass enclosure, the third fixed at the railing with another night-vision system. Although he couldn't be certain, there also may have been a fourth stationed on the ground below.

Lyons moved out in another half crouch. After pausing briefly to mark his position in relation to the waiting jeep, he continued at a run-walk until he reached the door of her hut. Instinct told him to simply kick it in, but he finally decided that he couldn't risk the noise.

Once again it was very dark inside her hut. She was curled in a ball on the cot, but when Lyons finally whispered her name, she immediately rose to face him.

"It's time," he said softly. "Do you understand, Molly? It's time to go."

She nodded, glancing past him to the open door, then reaching for a duffle coat. "Do I need...."

He shook his head. "There isn't time."

He felt her shivering as they eased out of the doorway, then felt her clinging very tightly to his arm. As they moved along the path beneath the Joshua trees, he felt her trembling again as if suddenly terrified of the shadows around them.

She wasn't watching the shadows, however. She was watching the soldier fixed on the gravel below the tower.

Lyons slipped his arm around her shoulder and pressed her face to his chest. "Don't move," he whispered. "Don't talk and don't move." Then very slowly slipping his hand beneath his windbreaker, he closed his fingers around the butt of his .45 auto.

"You got a problem, soldier?" No trace of emotion, not a shred of concern.

The guard responded with a quick glance to the tower above, then released the safety on his M-16. Although Lyons couldn't recall the man's name, he remembered him well enough from the obstacle course and the hand-to-hand mat: a nasty infighter from Paris, Texas, with a genuinely vicious streak.

"I'm afraid I'm going to have to ask you to step away from the girl, sir, and get down on your knees," the soldier said. Lyons did not respond. "I'm serious, sir. Step away from the girl and get on down, or I'm just going to have to cut you down.''

At least seven seconds passed before Lyons released the girl, and eased her away...seven seconds to contemplate killing an American in uniform. He thought about what they had done to Harold Gibb and tried to feed on the outrage. He thought about what they had done to Harwood and tried to feed on the indignation. He thought about Stack and that punk who had tried to waste him on the mat. He thought about Molly and the horror she must have experienced.

Yet, in the end, it was not an emotional call; it was a purely tactical one. Although the soldier's index finger remained firmly fixed on the trigger, his gaze had suddenly shifted left to the girl. Lyons, in turn, shifted his weight slightly to the right. Then dropping to his knees and hunching his back, he squeezed the .45 beneath his windbreaker. He squeezed with his whole hand, focusing on the soldier's chest, knowing full well that anything less than a dead center shot would probably cost him his life. As the weapon exploded beneath the black Gore-Tex and the soldier rose into the air with the impact, Lyons squeezed off a second round as insurance.

At least four seconds passed before anyone reacted—four stunned seconds wherein the soldier's chest continued to heave and his arms continued to jerk. Then as the girl began screaming and Blancanales started shouting from the jeep, six more shots broke from the tower.

Lyons dived into a roll, threw his arm around the girl's waist and continued rolling for cover in the shadows. He felt something slice above his right eye, but supposed that it was only a bit of plaster torn from the wall. He felt a spray of gravel on his back, then actually heard three high-velocity slugs whistle past his ear. But it wasn't until the spotlights fell, that he knew he wasn't going to make it.

The tower was equipped with two spotlights. But when they had converged, leaving Lyons and the girl cleanly etched against the brickwork, it almost seemed as if the whole world had suddenly burst into white flame.

Lyons staggered, glaring around him like a blinded bull vainly trying to shield the girl from the shots that he knew would follow. Yet when shots finally broke, it wasn't from the tower.

Lyons heard before he saw... heard the strained roar of the jeep closing in from beyond the lights, heard Blancanales shouting above the squealing tires. Then he heard the rhythmical crack of the jeep-mounted 50s, and what may have been the frantic scream of a guard hurling into a free-fall.

The tower seemed to disintegrate in stages, first imploding as Blancanales continued working the 50s from the back of the jeep, then exploding as Schwarz opened from behind the wheel with his H&K. There was another agonized scream as the spotlights shattered, leaving Lyons cloaked in blackness again. Then gazing up to the bullet-riddled tower, he actually caught a glimpse of another falling guard—the spine arched at an impossible angle, the arms outstretched as if poised for flight, the head back and the mouth wide.

In the end it seemed that everyone was shouting at once. Someone, probably Schwarz, kept yelling, "Let's go! Let's go!" Blancanales kept asking, "Where's the girl? Where's the girl?" Finally, as Lyons yanked the girl to her feet and shoved her into the jeep, he also heard the hoarse shout of another guard across the yard.

At least eight slugs glanced off the gravel as Schwarz punched the jeep into gear and tromped on the accelerator. Closer to the perimeter there were more shots: heavy shells from twin M-60s mounted in an outlying bunker, sprays of NATO specification rounds from another H&K.

Beyond the gates, however, where the road plunged into a deeper blackness and the mountains stood out like humped whales against the sky, there were no sounds at all except for the whistling wind.

13

Colonel Stack slammed a flattened hand to the wall, and squeezed his eyes shut. Behind him Corporal Harris and a security specialist named Billy Trask remained at mute attention, listening to the steady drip of coffee on the linoleum. The wall-mounted .45 now lay on the floor amid fragments of glass and wood—a further indication of the colonel's mood.

"All right." Stack finally sighed. "Why don't you just give it to me from the top."

Still not yet midnight, the colonel had been sound asleep when Harris had awakened him. Although he didn't bother dressing, he had nonetheless strapped on a side arm.

"Apparently it started with an entry to this office," Harris began. "When one of the sentries attempted to stop the perpetrator, he was beaten about the face and body and stuffed into a Dumpster."

"And then?"

"Then they moved in on the motor pool, confined two more sentries in handcuffs and made off with an armed vehicle."

"But not before abducting Miss Meekin, correct?"

"Yes, sir. Not before abducting Miss Meekin."

From the wall Stack moved to the window, pressing his palms against the cold glass and gazing out to the darting shadows of his men.

"What about casualties?" he breathed.

"I'm afraid we lost four, sir. Three on the southeast tower, one on the quad below it."

"And in exchange?"

Harris bit his lower lip. "We're not sure. That is, the perimeter bunker reports a delivery of at least thirty rounds, but there was no visual indication of damage infliction."

"Which basically means they got clean away, doesn't it?"

"Yes, sir."

Then suddenly turning from the window, Stack shouted, "Well, that's not okay in my book! You understand, Corporal? That just ain't acceptable!"

There was another taut silence as Stack pressed his palms to his desk and stared down at the remains of the shattered coffee cup.

Finally taking a deep breath and turning his gaze to Trask, he said, "Tell me about the wind, Sergeant."

Trask responded with a vaguely dazed stare. "The wind, sir?"

"Are we in a position to put up choppers or not?"

Trask stole a quick glance at Harris, who then shook his head. "No, sir. Not at least without risking a slam-dunk into the hills."

"And past the hills?"

Trask stole another quick glance at Harris, who again shook his head. "We'd still be taking a hell of a chance of losing one in the wind sheer."

Stack took another deep breath as if to inhale this data. "All right, then we'll just have take them on the ground," he said, briefly shutting his eyes.

"Yes, sir. Ground pursuit, sir, we can give you. In fact, ground pursuit is ready to launch as of right now."

"Then I suggest you launch that ground pursuit, Sergeant. I suggest you get your ass in a jeep, and launch that ground pursuit without delay."

"Yes, sir."

"And, Sergeant?"

"Sir?"

"I don't care how you do it, and I don't care who gets hurt. I just want the scalps. Is that clear? I just want you to launch that ground pursuit and collect me some scalps. Now!"

It was not until thirteen minutes after the hour that Trask and Harris actually moved out, leading a column of four weapons-mounted Jeep CJ-8s and three R-2 2.5 Gorgona fighting vehicles. They then lost another six or seven minutes attempting to determine which route their quarry had taken, and naturally the windblown sand didn't help matters at all.

LYONS TOLD SCHWARZ to pull off the road and stop the jeep. Although his initial instinct had simply been to put as much distance as possible between his party and the compound, it was now time to determine a slightly more original course of action. So against all apparent logic, he told Schwarz to pull into the shadows of the sandstone cliffs and stop the jeep.

It was by now nineteen minutes before midnight. The wind, which had kept the choppers off their back, had abated slightly, but still remained fierce on the flatlands. The girl, wearing only jeans and a Phil Collins promotional T-shirt beneath Schwarz's nylon jacket, was still shivering. The moon was once more obscured by clouds.

"Far as I can figure," Blancanales said, examining a map under the spray of his Mag-Lite, "we're just about three miles shy of the highway."

"We haven't got the speed for the highway," Schwarz mumbled. "They'll eat us alive on the open road."

"He's right. That's where they got me the first time," Molly Meekin whispered from the rear of the jeep.

But Lyons, who had already spent a fair amount of time figuring speeds and distances, merely shook his head. "What's going to kill us," he said, "is trying to fight them out here. Our only chance is to make it into the city."

They heard echoes of what was possibly an approaching half-track, but was actually only the wind sounding through the chaparral. There were also the occasional forms of darting animals: coyotes, jackrabbits, possibly deer. Then without warning, like the sudden crack of dry thunder, four F-15s streaked overhead.

When it was quiet again, Schwarz eased the jeep back onto the road with a heavy sigh. "All right then," he said, "let's head to Albuquerque. Get ourselves a couple of rooms at Hojo's and book the red-eye out of here. Nothing simpler."

By the time they reached the Wolf's Tooth pass, however, there were definitely headlights along the ridge above.

TRASK REMOVED THE LENS CAP from the AN/PVS-4 Star-lite scope and laid it on the seat. He then switched on the intensifier and scanned the road below. Although the scope had been fitted with an M-16 mount, Trask used it like the infrared pocket scopes he had used in Vietnam: his feet braced against the dashboard, his elbows braced against his knees, his heart beating faster and faster in anticipation of the kill.

"I ever tell you about air sports over the Highlands?" he asked.

"No." Harris said, knowing that Trask would tell the story regardless of what he said in reply.

"Well, dig it. You're like maybe right over the trees, just cruising along in a Huey behind an M-60. All of sudden there's like maybe fifteen or twenty dinks below you, working the rice fields or something. So what do you do?"

Harris shook his head with a short sigh. "I don't know, sir. What do you do?"

"Open up those flexies and let 'em pee. Because either way you got them pegged, right? Because if they start running that means they're trying to evade you, which means that they're Charlie. And if they just stand there and wave that means that they're trying to mess your head up, which also means they're Charlie. So either way, you got it covered, right? I mean either way you just opened up those flexies and let 'em pee."

Harris nodded, but said nothing. He knew that Trask would continue to talk for a while.

"So anyway, one day this reporter comes to the base camp," Trask continued. "He's like from *Time Magazine* or something, right? And he's asking me about the action, right? He's asking about what's been going down along the perimeters, what's been going down in the hamlets. The usual stuff. So I start telling him about the air sports and suddenly he cuts me off and says, 'Wait a minute, soldier, are you telling me that you've actually been shooting women and children?' So I say, 'Sure.' And then he says, 'Well, how can you do something like that?' And so I say, 'It's easy. You just don't lead 'em so much.' Get it? You just don't lead 'em so much."

Then although Harris had heard the story at least a dozen times before and knew it wasn't true, he still managed to force a little smile and laugh.

It was now eight minutes after midnight. Only nine minutes had passed since Harris had thought he'd seen something move below. He was suddenly no longer certain of anything ... not amid the shifting shadows and the dark forms of cacti.

"Maybe they took one of the fire roads," he said after another long silence. "Maybe they cut back at the rim and headed out through the brush."

Trask shook his head. "No, they're down there. I can feel it. I can feel it."

There was a surge of static from the radio, then the watery voice of a corporal in one of the Gorgonas behind them. There were cries of another coyote and what may have been another rabbit darting between the waves of chaparral. Finally shifting that Starlite scope to the darker ground below the pass, Trask suddenly whispered, "Oh, yeah. Oh sweet baby, yeah."

Harris withdrew an NF-1 hand-held scope and scanned the same ground as Trask. At first he saw nothing except more shifting shadows, but he finally also caught a glimpse of a defined movement—a solid form against the shifting forms, a suggestion of a fender and those quad 50s.

"Maybe we can catch 'em on the slope," he said. "Skirt that ridge up there, and catch 'em on the slope."

But again Trask shook his head. "They're downwind of us. We start revving up the engines, and they'll hear us sure as shit."

"So what do you suggest?"

Trask laid down the Starlite scope, and picked up the radio mike. "I say we open up those flexies and let 'em pee," he smiled.

"I EVER TELL YOU about the Special Forces guys in the Highlands?" Blancanales asked.

Lyons shook his head.

"Spring '67. I pull a Special Forces assignment up near the border, which was pretty wild country. I walk into this little hamlet and all these Special Forces guys are standing around with shit-eating grins and hunting knives. I ask 'em what's happening, and they show me this VC they'd just skinned. I mean skinned him clean. So I said, 'Hey, what's the point?' And you know what they told me? They told me there was no point. They just felt like skinning a VC.''

It was now sixteen minutes after midnight. Having caught a second glimpse of those headlights on the ridge, Schwarz had pulled off the road again and cut the engine. But although Lyons had also withdrawn a Starlite device—one of the smaller second generation pocket scopes—he could no longer see anything beyond shivering spears of Spanish saber and creosote.

''Maybe we should meet them on foot,'' Schwarz said after another long silence. ''Maybe we should split up, take those antitankers and hit from the high bush on foot.''

Lyons shook his head. ''Not until we find out what we're facing,'' he said. ''I mean, we start tramping around the brush now, we could find ourselves cut off and pinned down.''

''He's right,'' Molly whispered softly from the back.

In addition to their H&Ks and assorted ammunition, Blancanales had also managed to get his hands on two RPG-7 antitank grenade launchers. But they were not weapons that either he or Lyons were particularly familiar with. And both men knew that given the speed of the Gorgona armored vehicle, a hit would be tricky.

''Well, we sure as hell can't just sit here and wait for them to cut us off from below,'' Schwarz replied.

''He's right,'' Blancanales added. ''We sit here much longer, and we could find ourselves boxed in real good.''

''So what do you suggest?'' Lyons asked.

"Well, I don't know," Blancanales breathed, "but I'm starting to think that maybe we should...*get the hell out of here right now!*"

Four distinct bursts from a Gorgona's 7.62 mm turret gun cut into the brush around them.

"Go!" TRASK SHOUTED into the mike. "Go! Go! Go!" Then bracing himself against the rear seat, he squeezed off another three rounds from the turret gun.

All around him the blackened bush was suddenly alive with tracers and sweeping headlights as his pursuit team lurched into action. There may have also been incoming fire from below, but he wasn't about to stop and assess it...not now, not when he virtually had the bastards in his sights.

"Cut back to that fire road!" he shouted to Harris behind the wheel. "Cut back to that fire road and I'll catch 'em from behind."

But amid a smear of sweeping headlights and cracking autofire, Harris was no longer even certain where the main road was.

He cursed as the Gorgona plunged into walls of thick brush, and something large and hard thudded against the right front fender. Dry foliage exploded against the windshield and the steering wheel bucked in his hands.

"Where the hell are you going?" Trask shouted, bucking in the rear seat and squeezing off another six or seven blind rounds. "They're over there."

"Where?"

"There!"

But swerving back onto the fire road and easing to a stop, all Harris saw was vast blackness.

"You stupid shit," Trask said. "You fucking lost them."

ONE BY ONE the pursuit team also cut their engines in order to wait and listen.

A long white beam from a jeep-mounted spotlight penetrated the chaparral. A frustrated burst from a 7.62 mm Gorgona's turret gun sprayed the spears of cactus and Joshua below the ridge. Finally, from no more than a hundred yards away, Able Team heard someone say, "Shit!"

"Okay, so they're pissed." Blancanales smiled. "If nothing else, at least we managed to piss them off."

"Why don't you take a look through the scope?" Lyons whispered from the back of the jeep.

Blancanales picked up the Starlite scope from between his knees, switched it on and scanned through the spears of cactus to the ridge above. But in the end, he simply shook his head. "Nothing."

"So maybe we got lucky," Schwarz said. "Maybe most of them took a wrong turn on that fire road back there."

"I wouldn't count on it," Lyons replied.

At some point in the last few minutes, the girl had slipped off the seat and onto the floor. She had shut her eyes and begun to cry. Now and again, Lyons reached down and stroked her hair or pressed a hand to her shoulder. But it didn't seem to do much good.

"All right, how about we do something like this?" Blancanales said suddenly into the windy silence. "How about I take one of those antitankers and stalk them on foot for a while?"

Lyons reached across the seat, picked up the Starlite scope and began to scan the low ground behind them. Apart from the stock-still form of an owl, however, he saw nothing.

"We're talking about one hell of a lot of ground out there, Pol," Lyons finally said.

Blancanales shrugged. "So I'll stick to the road. Blow me a couple of jeeps, maybe one of those armored cars and generally unleash a little havoc until you guys pick me up at the highway. What do you say?''

"I like it," Schwarz replied.

"All right," Lyons breathed. "Except instead of you out there, it's going to be me."

"I KNEW GUYS LIKE THAT in Nam," Trask said softly, more to himself than to Harris. "Real heroes. Real ball breaking heroes. Only problem with them was they weren't team players. Always volunteering for solo work. Always sneaking around in the night. Looks good on paper, but no real *effectiveness*. You understand what I'm saying? No real *effectiveness*."

Harris put down the night-vision system and sank a little deeper behind the wheel of the Gorgona. Ever since Trask had ordered him to cut the engine, he had been forced to listen to a steady stream of fragmented discourse. At one point, after catching a glimpse of Trask's eyes in the rearview mirror, it occurred to him that the man was probably insane; and that even if Trask had died right then and there, the man's jaws would continue to work for at least another hour.

"Maybe we should move back onto the main road," he finally suggested for want of anything else.

Typically, however, Trask merely shook his head and smirked. "You want to move back to the main road, huh? Well, let me tell you something about that kind of thinking, soldier. That is exactly the kind of thinking that those bastards expect from us. That is exactly the kind of bullshit that they will *expect* us to employ."

Trask reached across the seat, picked up the scope that Harris had just laid aside and began to scan the ground below the road. There were cries of another owl in the brush to their left, cactus spears rustling in the wind to their right.

After another three or four minutes of scanning, however, it was obvious that Trask hadn't caught sight of them, either.

"So what do we do now, sir?" Harris asked, mainly because he couldn't resist needling his commander.

Trask laid down the scope and slid back behind the turret gun. "I'll tell you what we do, Corporal. We are going to employ what those bastards are unable to employ— teamwork. We are going to get on the radio, and instruct our support to move out in a concerted and organized manner, and then we are going to squeeze those bastards in a pincer. Is that clear?"

"Yes, sir."

"Then I suggest you pick up that radio and relay my orders."

"Yes, sir."

But even before Harris was able to detach his hand from the wheel and reach across the dash, the night came alive again with autofire.

LYONS SQUEEZED OFF another two-second burst, then sank back into the chaparral and inserted another magazine into his H&K. Although he had also packed four M-26 grenades, he had finally decided against the antitank launcher—too bulky. Besides, although the Gorgona featured a bullet-resistant windshield and windows, the tires were still vulnerable—one more reason why the United States Army continued to consider contracts for a high-speed armored vehicle.

Lyons had counted three jeeps and two Gorgonas before sliding deeper into the brush. Although his first burst had probably hit nothing beyond a few Joshua trees, it had definitely startled the enemy. He was now at least able to determine their position from the frenzied sweep of search-lights and the sudden revving of engines.

He slipped to his belly as another long beam of white light knifed through the brush above him. Lyons ducked his head as three savage bursts from mounted 50-calibers sliced through the mounds of chaparral around him. Then inching forward through a veritable tunnel of cactus, he eased back up to a firing position and sighted into the light.

There had been moments, crawling through this tangled scrub, when Lyons had virtually forgotten what kind of enemy he was facing; it all came back to him now. Wedged in a streambed with his H&K fixed on the black silhouette of a soldier behind a spotlight...he suddenly couldn't keep his mind from it any longer. Those men out there weren't just another third world terrorist team; they were Americans, members of this nation's armed forces, veterans of the same sort of dirty little wars that he and his Able Team colleagues had fought. And now he was about to blow them away.

He waited, holding his breath to steady his hands, then even shutting his eyes to clear his mind. I could have been one of them, he thought. Could have been recruited off the rebound from a job in Honduras or Sri Lanka, briefed en route from an outlying base and then stationed at the Wolf's Tooth. Sure, things might have looked a little weird from time to time, but in the end you just follow orders. In the end you just keep your mouth shut, your eyes open and do what you're told.

He opened his eyes and slowly switched the selector switch from a three-burst mode to full automatic. I definitely could have been one of those guys out there, he thought. Me, Schwarz, Blancanales—we might have been out there right now, tracking three clowns in a stolen jeep.

But then he thought about the girl, thought about what she must have been through, what she must have seen. Then suddenly recalling a distinct impression of her tearstained face, he finally squeezed the trigger.

TRASK HAD BEEN DESCRIBING another of his search and destroy adventures from 1968, something about nailing an enemy patrol with M-60s. Harris had been riding the brake, frantically trying to maneuver the Gorgona over a flood-eroded trail. The driver of the second Gorgona had been screaming over the radio, literally screaming that he was receiving enemy fire. Then suddenly swinging the wheel hard left, all Harris saw was the number two jeep.

The jeep, manned by Corporal Lester Madison and Private Roger Hollis, had been closing from the lower fire trail. Although Harris couldn't see Madison's face behind the wheel, he definitely saw Hollis—a mean boonierat from Arkansas—crouched behind the spotlight.

"You're going the wrong way!" Trask began shouting. "Can't you see? You're going the wrong way!"

But all Harris finally saw was Hollis's head and shoulders disintegrating in the spray of white light.

Apparently Hollis screamed twice, first as the NATO specification rounds began glancing off the spotlight mount, then again as those same rounds began shredding his flesh. In the end he must have been hit at least six times before he finally sailed off the back of the jeep and into the spears of cactus.

"We have contact!" Harris began shouting. "I repeat. We have contact!"

Yet the only answer was another long burst of automatic fire from the brush.

At least fifteen rounds glanced off the armor plate surrounding the Gorgona—fifteen clean shots that sounded like basketballs bouncing on tin. Harris responded with a hard turn right, but only succeeded in catching six more rounds across the side plate.

"Hold her steady!" Trask shouted. "Hold her steady. I got 'em in my sights!"

But when Trask finally let loose with that turret gun, all Harris saw were more shredded spears of cactus billowing in the headlights.

BELOW THE FIRE ROAD lay a grove of snow-fed cottonwoods, desert willows and rushes. The ground was laced with a network of shallow ruts—further evidence of water. There was also more creosote here, burr sage and Spanish saber. For at least seven minutes Lyons remained absolutely motionless among this vegetation. Then finally slipping into one of the tiny alluvial furrows, he gradually started forward again. He tried to keep his mind on the practical problems—on the terrain, the distances, and the various lines of fire—ultimately there was really no avoiding it: he was fighting a contingent of American soldiers and they probably didn't even know why.

He paused where the ground fell away to a broader alluvial wash. From here, he had a fairly clean view of the landscape: the long waves of chaparral extending to the highway, the lunar forms of rock below and the distant lights of the city. He also had a fairly clean view of his enemy: six pairs of headlights closing in a long arc from the fire road.

He waited until the pursuit team had drawn in line with the cottonwoods before picking his target. He waited until he could actually see the outline of the driver behind the wheel of the first jeep in the rank. Then bracing his back against the side of the rut, and sighting along the spears of

Spanish saber, Lyons waited another fifteen or twenty seconds.

Initially he aimed for the engine, because stopping the vehicle would ultimately serve the same purpose as killing them. But even before he began to squeeze the trigger, he saw the spotlights swing around. He saw the bulky outline of a gunner, shouting above the straining engine. He saw the black eyes of a driver growing suddenly wide with horror or excitement. He saw the headlights turning to face him, and he finally fired for the windshield.

Glass and blood, briefly glowing in the spotlight, exploded in a circular cloud. Another frantic scream rose above the engine's whine as the jeep swerved left, hurling the gunner into the cactus spears. Lyons fired again as a second jeep swung in from behind the clustered creosote. There were more screams from a driver, quivering under a spray of bullets; more screams from an engine straining with a shattered piston. Then finally turning at the sound of something lumbering through the brush not fifteen feet away, his eyes locked onto the eyes of the bulky gunner from the first jeep.

The soldier was young, no more than twenty; and although the eyes were alive with fury, the innocence was unmistakable. I know that kid, Lyons thought vaguely. I faced him on the mats, showed him how to reverse a choke-hold and how to sweep a leg. He also recalled having showed the kid how to load and fire a Browning P-53 on a roll, which was exactly what the kid was doing now.

Lyons shouted before he squeezed the trigger again, actually shouted the kid's name: *Stanley!* Then sensing a flicker of recognition, he shouted it again: *Staaanley, don't do it!* But this time the Browning had already started flashing, and Lyons couldn't wait any longer.

He fired as he dropped to his belly, fired with a long burst to the kid's chest. Then watching the kid shivering with impact, he fired again at the face. The kid seemed to hang in the air for at least a second, his left arm stiff at his side, his right arm reaching for the sky. Then literally bursting with blood, he collapsed back into those vicious spears of cactus.

Lyons fired three more quick bursts at the ridge before finally withdrawing again. He fired in a wide arc, possibly blowing a tire on one of the Gorgonas, possibly hitting nothing but the afterglow of headlights. Finally, yanking out the empty clip, he hurled himself back into the black coils of sage and chaparral.

It was suddenly oddly still and quiet. Although the air above him came alive again with darting spotlights and random fire from those quad 50s, he was finally left with a sense of absolute peace. A horned owl, intrigued by his presence, watched from a high branch above. A coyote, frightened by the echo of gunfire, whimpered from far across the gorge. Even when he finally heard those Gorgonas descending from the high ground, obviously swinging around to trap him, he still couldn't seem to bring himself to move.

HARRIS SWUNG THE WHEEL in a slow arc, letting the Gorgona find its way over the rutted ground. Fifty yards to his left a second Gorgona followed his lead, while the two surviving jeeps closed from the opposite direction. Through it all, Trask continued whispering from behind the turret guns, "Now we got him. Now we got that bastard right where we want him." Now and again he also whispered things in Vietnamese, snatches of phrases that still bounced around in his brain from the war.

There were four leafless cottonwoods at the end of the fire trail. Beyond the trees lay the black patch of bush where Harris had seen Stanley fall. It wasn't until he eased the Gorgona into the cactus patch, however, that he actually saw the body: grotesquely spread across the tiny spikes, the eyes still fixed on the stars, the top of the head blown clean away.

"Forget about him," Trask said. "Just keep driving and forget about him."

Harris slowed as they neared the darkest ends of the brush. Although there were several shadows that seemed to suggest a crouching man, suddenly nothing seemed particularly defined... not the indistinct shapes that may have been waiting in the brush, not the point of killing another man, not even the overall point of the Wolf's Tooth program.

"Figure it this way," Trask was saying. "We're the dogs, and he's the rabbit. Now, this guy might be one mean rabbit, but he's still just a rodent. And you know what we do to rodents, don't you? Huh, Corporal? You know what we do to rodents?"

But beyond the spray of the headlights and the longer sweep of the spotlight, Harris wasn't sure that he knew anything anymore....

Except that maybe, just maybe, Lyons wasn't alone. That maybe the slow shifting shadow actually meant that Schwarz or Blancanales had somehow brought their jeep up, and was right now sighting down the barrels of that quad 50.

Then all that Harris knew was that something was pounding on the side of the armored door, repeatedly pounding like a jackhammer. He was also certain that something was wrong with the steering, and that possibly the right front tire had blown. And he knew that at least six 50-caliber slugs had slammed into the number three jeep to his left, shattering the windshield and shredding the driver to a bloody pulp.

"We're in trouble!" Harris screamed. "Real *trouble*!"

But Trask only screamed in reply as the Gorgona lurched out of control as two more slugs shattered the bullet-resistant glass.

BLANCANALES SWUNG THE quad 50 in a long arc and squeezed another twenty rounds into the skidding Gorgona. He had never been particularly impressed with the R-2 2.5 command car. Nor had he been particularly impressed with Trask's attack formation...which was ultimately why he couldn't resist bringing up the jeep and unleashing that quad 50.

Bursts of return fire broke from the ridge and Schwarz began shouting something about a second Gorgona. But by now Blancanales had already locked on to a jeep, fixing on the driver and finally squeezing out another twenty rounds. There were more screams of metal, mixing with the cries of men, and at least two bloody forms briefly appeared in a spotlight before crumpling back into the blackness.

"Where's Carl?" Schwarz was shouting. "Where's Carl?"

"Here!" Lyons shouted back, scrambling from the brush as another burst of fire cracked from the ridge.

"Then let's go!" Schwarz yelled. "Let's go! Let's go! Let's go!"

Blancanales sprayed the high ground with another long burst as Lyons leaped into the jeep. Then firing again as Schwarz tromped down on the accelerator, he caught a glimpse of a second driver crumpling behind the wheel of a skidding jeep. But, although he may have had a clean shot at Trask as the man scrambled from the crippled Gorgona, he did not fire.

14

Lyons told Schwarz to dump the jeep eighteen miles down the highway. It was now about two o'clock in the morning. Molly Meekin, traumatized by the horror she had witnessed, had grown very quiet.

They abandoned the jeep in a culvert outside of the city. They made some effort to conceal it with leaves and branches torn from surrounding foliage, but Lyons did not expect that the vehicle would remain undiscovered for long. He knew that it was likely the jeep would be discovered by kids—ten or twelve-year-olds in jeans and T-shirts, kids who secretly longed for adventure every waking minute of their lives. For that reason Lyons ordered Schwarz to remove the firing pins from the machine gun, and that he dump the remaining ammunition into the storm drain. There was no point in killing innocent children.

Half a mile beyond the culvert Schwarz spotted two vehicles that he felt would serve as appropriate transportation to take them into the city: a beige Toyota and a white Volkswagen Rabbit. Not only were the vehicles easy to hot-wire, but they were common enough not to attract undue attention. Then Blancanales spotted the black Trans Am parked outside a luxury apartment complex.

"You ever driven one of those things?" he asked Schwarz with a slow smile.

"Yeah, so?" Schwarz replied.

"So if we're going to steal a car, let's at least steal something with cruise control and enough muscle to get us where we want to go. You understand what I'm saying here? Let's at least steal something with a decent sound system."

In the end, however, they only drove the Trans Am about nine miles before leaving it in a parking lot adjacent to the airport. Then, of course, rather than boarding a plane, they simply checked into the local Howard Johnson's using an American Express Gold Card in the name of Edward R. Thordike.

IT WAS NEARLY DAWN when Lyons and Blancanales finally turned their attention to the material that Schwarz had taken from Colonel Stack's office. Molly Meekin had finally managed to fall asleep, while Schwarz more or less dozed in a chair by the window. They had decided it was safer for Molly to stay under their protection than for her to return home.

They began with what Lyons called "the broad view." After a cursory study of the pages, Blancanales sketched a crude map of the nation's capital on a sheet of paper torn from the wastebasket lining. Ashtrays, pens and bathroom glasses were then used to represent the various Wolf's Tooth units named in the report. An L.L. Bean field watch was used to keep the time. A bit of string, torn from the venetian blind, was used to calculate the distances.

"You ever play these kinds of games in the service?" Lyons asked.

Blancanales shrugged. "I never played them, but I studied them."

"Then tell me what you see. Putting aside everything else that's happened and just looking at the game board, tell me what you see."

Blancanales took another sip of coffee, his third or fourth cup since checking into the hotel. He traced a finger along the edge of his crude map and leafed through the first six pages of the game report. "I see a classic seize and hold maneuver," he said. "I see a perfectly coordinated seize and hold."

Lyons nodded, also running a hand along the edge of that crude map. "Exactly, seize and hold."

He rose from his chair and stepped to the window. Now technically dawn, the sky was still black with clouds and slanting rain. There was a fair amount of traffic on the highway, however, and he counted at least three vehicles that might have come from the Wolf's Tooth Complex.

"I kind of get the feeling that it would happen like this," Lyons said at last. "It's an ordinary spring morning. Probably a Wednesday or Thursday, a day when there are full sessions in the House and Senate. Following a series of simulated terrorist attacks in four or five cities across the nation, the Wolf's Tooth units move into action. Although they're supposedly on orders from the White House, in fact the White House knows nothing about it. In fact, they're following orders issued by the Pentagon. After supposedly meeting armed resistance in, say, the ghettos, they move into what is called a defensive posture around the Hill. Finally, and supposedly in response to massive foreign-backed domestic insurrection, they physically move in on the government. I mean they literally take it over."

Blancanales picked up the game report and flipped to a section entitled, "Psyops I and II: Individual State Security, and Public Opinion Management." Among the notations below were references to a "Simulated Media Alert," an "Active and Passive Television Response," and "Immediate Insured Network Cooperation." What most intrigued Blancanales, however, was something called

"Popular Credibility Parameters," which seemed to include an entirely new definition of democracy.

"Think of it as any third world coup," Lyons continued. "The numbers may be a lot bigger, but the basic approach is the same. You physically take control of the capital, and then start shooting those previously in command."

"Yeah, but how the hell do they expect to keep the lid on it? How the hell do they expect to keep the Press from blowing the whistle before they get themselves stabilized?"

"The Press can only report what they see, and they only see what they're told to see. Besides, I don't think Ted Koppel would be willing to throw his life away for a few minutes of glory on the air."

"All right, but what about Mr. Average American at Anytown, USA? How the hell do they expect to control two hundred million of those guys?"

Lyons shrugged, turning his gaze from the highway to the seemingly endless ranks of suburban homes where lights were only now being turned on in the kitchens and bedrooms.

"It's a simple matter of firepower," he said at last. "When the Constitution was framed there were certain safeguards inserted in order to protect the people from just this kind of event. The right to bear arms, for example, was based upon the fact that in 1780 weapons technology was such that you really couldn't raise an army that was much stronger than a militia group. I mean, a musket was a musket and almost anyone could cast a cannon. Today, that's just not the case. Today, even three or four hundred thousand armed civilians are no match for what the Pentagon can throw at them."

"So what do we do?" Schwarz asked, finally rousing himself from his nap and reaching for a cup of lukewarm coffee. "Assuming you're right, and they've got all the cards, what kind of choices do we have?"

"I'm not sure." Lyons sighed.

THEY WAITED UNTIL SEVEN in the evening before moving out again. Although the winds had subsided, the air remained cold with the rain. Having booked at least a dozen flights to various cities around the world, Lyons and Molly then caught a taxi to the airport. Exactly thirty minutes later Schwarz and Blancanales followed by bus. At one of the airport gift shops, Lyons purchased three or four sweatshirts with various college logos, three or four pairs of sunglasses, a baseball cap and a cowboy hat. He also bought a raincoat for Molly and a cheap camera to wear around his neck. Although these "disguises" would probably not pass a close inspection, Lyons wasn't worried. He knew that it was a casual glance from the corner of an eye, or the long-range scanning of a crowd that would initially expose them. If it ever came down to a close inspection, he had told the others, they would be finished.

They boarded in pairs at the last call: first Lyons and Molly, then Schwarz and Blancanales. Although Lyons had told the girl that they would be safe the moment they boarded the plane, in fact he knew that the opposite was true. From the moment they stepped onto the plane to the moment the plane left the ground, he knew they were vulnerable. He knew there would be no place to run, no place to hide and no place to maneuver for a fight.

In the end, however, the only apparent mishap before leaving the ground was an unscheduled change of the in-flight movie. Instead of the Eddie Murphy comedy, the passengers would have to put up with a twenty-year-old

Paramount Pictures classic from the TWA on-board library: *Seven Days in May*, starring Kirk Douglas, Burt Lancaster, Fredric March and Ava Gardner.

15

A secret, Lyle Severson used to tell his students on those rare occasions when he lectured at the CIA's training facility at Camp Perry, was rather like an onion: one could never hope to fully grasp it, until one had peeled away at least a dozen layers of surrounding lies.

Although Severson had not seriously thought about this analogy in years, it was very much on his mind as he waited in the shadows of the Lincoln Memorial for his sometime friend and occasional enemy in the KGB. A river wind had left him chilled to the bone, and he was scared...for the first time since it had begun, he was genuinely scared.

It was actually a beautiful evening, with a faintly orange glow to the rippling surface of the Reflecting Pool and a deeper blue to the sky above Capitol Hill. But by the time Colonel Gregor Panov arrived, the moon glowed to the left of the Washington Monument—a strangely crimson moon that almost suggested the Ides of March.

Over the years Severson and Panov had often met to unofficially discuss matters of mutual concern: terrorism, Persian Gulf hostilities, the exchange of captured spies. Naturally, however, neither man had ever been entirely open with the other, and the give and take of information had always been a complicated process. But when Severson had first received word that Panov wished to meet again, he immediately suspected the KGB colonel was going to speak with entirely unprecedented candor. To a degree that suspicion was confirmed the moment Severson saw the colonel ascend the steps of the Memorial. It was in the man's eyes, in his walk and in the way he grasped Severson's hand.

"So, my friend, here we are again—*perestroika* in action."

Although Russian to the core, eight years in Washington under cover of the Soviet Cultural Mission had given Panov an undeniably American manner. His gray flannel suit, for example, was from Brooks Brothers. His brown suede wing tips were from Cole-Haan. His tie was an Ivy League rep and his watch was naturally a Rolex. There was still a trace of an accent, but only when he was nervous or excited.

"I suppose I might as well get directly to the point," he said. Then glancing over his shoulder out of habit, and shrugging his heavy shoulders, he continued. "I'm afraid that something very bad may be happening, something very bad for the both of us."

They receded deeper into the shadows, more or less directly below Lincoln's compassionate gaze. Although the surrounding lawns were deserted, two kites were bobbing and weaving above the trees.

"Why don't you just start from the beginning?" Severson said.

"Very well," Panov nodded, "from the beginning. Eight days ago, we received word—it doesn't matter how—that a certain general attached to the Pentagon will soon order a Red Alert. This is to be a true Red Alert, not a test. Although this condition is normally a response to a foreign threat, the Pentagon will claim that national security is at stake because of a domestic threat."

Up until now Severson had focused his gaze on the far ground—on the stark outline of the Washington Monument and on the dimmer outline of the Hill. But finally turning to face the colonel, he gazed deeply into the man's eyes.

"I want you to be straight with me, Panov," he said softly. "I don't care what it costs me in the long run, but this time you've got to be straight."

Panov nodded again, suddenly looking very Russian with his doughy features and bushy eyebrows. "I am being straight with you, my friend. There is soon to be a general Red Alert of all United States military forces, but the hidden purpose of this Red Alert is to allow the takeover of your nation."

"When, Gregor? When?" he asked, looking directly into the colonel's eyes.

"Soon, my friend, soon."

Panov jammed his hands in his pockets and turned to gaze out to the lengthening shadows of trees and the darkening rooftops of the skyline.

"This is not a rumor," Panov said after a long silence. "This is not Soviet disinformation designed to trick Western intelligence. This is real, my friend. This is real information from Soviet sources."

Severson laid a hand on the colonel's shoulder. "What kind of source?" he asked softly. Panov did not reply. "Look, I don't care if you've got a placement in the Pentagon. I'm just trying to assess the reliability," Severson continued.

Panov remained silent, then finally nodded with a long sigh. "Very well, I will tell you. The information is not from human placement. The information is from intercepted cables."

"Cables between whom?"

"Between certain high ranking Pentagon generals and somewhat lower ranking generals abroad. Also, as you know, we are in a position to monitor various military activities by spy satellite and we are therefore certain that something is not right in your country."

There was another long silence as Panov scanned the banks of the Reflecting Pool, and Severson gazed back into the Lincoln Memorial.

"You must understand that I tell you this as both a friend and a patriot of my country," Panov said at last. "You follow my meaning here? I tell you as both a friend and a Soviet patriot, because although recently our two countries have made great progress on the road to world peace and mutual affinity, I now fear that all will be lost . . . all will be lost if these reactionary generals take control of your government. I also fear for you on a personal level. If these generals take control, you will be among the first to die."

Severson extended a hand to Panov's shoulder again, let it linger a moment, then finally let it fall away.

"How widespread were those military movements you referred to?" Severson asked.

Panov shrugged again, then shook his head. "Judging by the amount of cable traffic, I would have to say that portions of at least three branches of your military are involved in this coup: Army, Navy, Air Force."

"But not the entire command corps?"

"No, probably not the entire command. But in order to fight it, you must first determine who is loyal and who is not . . . which may not be an easy task."

They parted on the windswept lawns below the memorial.

"I'm not going to say that I owe you for this one," Severson sighed as they moved through the deepening shadows. "But by the same token, I'd like to say thanks."

Panov held up a hand. "Your thanks is not necessary, my friend. Indeed, I only wish that I could do more to help you."

"You mean like sending in a couple of Soviet battalions to preserve our democracy?" Severson smiled.

Panov also smiled, but only for a moment. "Don't think it hasn't crossed my mind, my friend."

IT WAS HALF PAST SIX in the evening when Severson returned to Langley...the slack hour between the day-shift's departure and the night-shift's arrival. Apart from the hollow clack of the coding machines and the high whine of shredders, the rooms were generally quiet. Only three or four analysts toiled behind their glass partitions. Only four or five security clerks watched from behind the banks of monitors.

In all Severson would spend almost nine hours that night trying to make sense of what was happening in the nation. He began with intercepts of cable traffic snatched from the National Security Agency, then turned again to the internal traffic between Company links and their opposite numbers in Defense. Finally, calling in a favor from counterintelligence, he began to focus on the individuals: Rambling Ray Doyle, Arthur Matoon Clancy and the sand sharks that ran between them.

16

It was just after seven o'clock in the evening when the generals arrived at the lodge. They arrived in rented vehicles that they drove themselves. A few carried briefcases. The rest carried nothing. None were in uniform. Through the eyes of a casual witness, this gathering might have suggested a poker party or an overnight golf junket. Yet there were no golf clubs, no potato chips and no beer.

Although the lodge may have originally been built to house hunters, most of the local game had been killed off years ago, and that which remained was now protected by a local ordinance. There were, however, reminders of the hunt throughout the building: a moose head above the massive stone hearth, heads of deer along the oak paneled walls, mounted Winchesters and a bearskin rug. There were also pheasants on the cocktail napkins that Robert Maloy distributed in order to protect the furniture, and tiny geese on the swizzle stick that Rambling Ray Doyle used to emphasize his opening remarks.

"I'm afraid we've got a little problem, gentlemen," he began, stabbing the swizzle stick into the air for emphasis. "Now I'm not saying it's anything to get excited about, but we definitely have ourselves a little problem."

The next to speak was Arthur Matoon Clancy. "I'm going to have to concur with Ray," he said. "I don't think we need to call out the reserves, but we most definitely need to discuss this thing, before it kicks us in the teeth."

Finally, and more or less deflating the tension in the room, a rangy Admiral named David Waugh Jones rose to his feet and laid an enormous hand on the mantle. "Well, if this is such a goddamn problem, then maybe one of you boys wouldn't mind filling me in on the details?"

At which point the fifth man present, a stocky Marine by the name of Albert Wright Duke, actually broke into laughter.

Maloy took the floor. As the junior officer, it was his duty to break bad news and he almost seemed to relish the job.

"As of yesterday at twenty-two hundred hours, we received word of a severe security problem at the Wolf's Tooth. Although the details are still a little sketchy, it seems that three temporary personnel broke into Stack's office and made off with one of the Game Reports. It also appears that they made off with the civilian hostage."

Two or three voices erupted in response, but typically the Marine Corps' carried the most volume. "What the hell do you mean they *made off* with one of the Game Reports?" Duke shouted.

"I mean, sir, that they stole it, sir."

"Which one?"

"The Capital Defense Games from April and May."

The Admiral spoke next, shaking his head and breathing through his teeth. "What do we know about the culprits?" he asked.

Doyle also sighed through clenched teeth. "Not a whole lot. Supposedly they were brought in as special instructors, but they're not exactly regular military."

"Then what exactly are they?" Duke asked.

"Well, they're sort of half breeds," Clancy replied. "They're sort of...well, sources say they call themselves Able Team."

"I guess the real question is, what the hell are we going to do about it?" Duke asked. "Because unless you boys have forgotten, that Capital Defense Game was critical and I mean *critical*."

Doyle rose to his feet, still toying with the swizzle stick. "The Game Report is an indicator," he said. "But in no way is it going to give them the whole picture."

"Even so," Clancy said, "I think we'd better start thinking about how we're going to get the toothpaste back in the tube...and fast."

"A security team *has* been launched," Maloy said. "We've also alerted some of the local agencies, and I'm trying to put a little pressure on the FBI."

"Well, you be damn careful, baby," Duke hissed. "You be real damn careful."

To which Clancy added, "Al's right. We make a federal case out of this and there's no telling what kind of questions people are going to start asking."

A second round of drinks was poured, and more of those cocktail napkins were distributed. There were also peanuts in a glass bowl but no one touched them.

"I'm not going to try to minimize the problem here," Doyle said, addressing the others from the hearth. "But at the same time, I don't think there's any need to panic. Essentially what we're talking about is a leak. We're taking on water. We've suffered a few casualties, but we're still afloat and we're still battle ready."

"But they also know our position," the admiral countered. "They know our position, and are obviously lining up their guns."

"Well, that's the whole point, isn't it?" said Clancy. "What can they throw at us? I mean really, what can they throw at us?"

"You want to wait around and find out?" Duke asked with a smirk.

"Exactly," the admiral said. "Do we want to wait around and find out?"

Doyle took another sip of brandy waiting for the questions to stop. Then finally withdrawing a notebook from his pocket, he turned to face the others again. "Now, I've been reviewing the logistics," he said, "and I think it's entirely possible to move up the timetable a little. Say, six weeks to strike day?"

"That's going to give my people a little headache," Clancy responded.

"Then break out the aspirin," Duke shot back. "Because Ray's right on the mark. We need to move up the strike day, catch 'em off guard, kick 'em in the teeth before they've got a chance to figure out what's happening."

"I've also been reviewing the tactical side of things and I think we might start looking at putting a little more power into our opening punch. Just something to knock them off their feet a little, create a broader shock factor."

"Well, if you're thinking about aircraft," Clancy interjected, "Then I'm going to have to put my foot down. Because once you start putting planes up there, ain't nobody in the country going to believe that this is some kind of civilian action."

"No, not aircraft," Doyle replied.

"Then what?" Duke asked.

"Gas," Doyle said. "A yellow-white cocktail of mustard, nerve and maybe a dose of hydrogen cyanide."

"Oh, shit," Jones began whispering.

"Like I said," Doyle added, "it's just to increase the panic factor a little. Throw them a curve they don't expect, and give us an opportunity to catch 'em with their pants down. I don't figure a particularly substantial increase in casualties, not in the long run."

"Well, I don't like it," the admiral said. "I don't like it one bit."

Then although there may have been one or two other protests, once again the voice of the Marine Corps essentially ended the debate.

"Gentlemen," Duke began, "I'm afraid that the time for soul-searching is over. Now, if Raymond here feels we need a little gas, then we need a little gas. Because unless you boys have forgotten, we are not going to be playing footsie out there. We are going to be removing a destructive, but nonetheless legally elected government. And although you may want to think of it as a patriotic necessity, you can be damned sure that that's not what they're going to call it if we fail. Fact is, they're going to call it treason—plain and simple treason against these United States. Now unless you boys have something else to say, I move that we adjourn this meeting so I can get myself home for dinner."

They parted on the gravel drive beneath a circle of leafless oaks. Although there were echoes of barking dogs in the distance, there were no indications of human life—no lights in the hills, no traffic on the road and no cries of children from the neighboring fields.

"Unless anyone has an objection," Doyle said as he led his party to their waiting vehicles, "I don't see any reason to meet again until strike day."

"What about the emergency contact procedure?" Clancy asked.

Doyle glanced at Maloy and Maloy shrugged. "Well, obviously you can always contact the general through my office in the event of an emergency, but frankly I don't anticipate any snags from here on out.''

"And what do you call the incident at the Wolf's Tooth?" Admiral Jones asked.

"Like I said," Doyle countered, "The Wolf's Tooth problem is contained. And unless I've seriously underestimated the opposition, I still don't think those Game Reports are going to tell them very much. In fact, I don't think those Game Reports are going to tell them anything at all.''

"And the girl?" Duke asked. "What is the girl going to tell them?''

"She's going to tell them that she wants to go home to Daddy. That's what she's going to tell them. Period.''

17

Molly Meekin took a deep breath and ran her finger along the spine of the Game Report.

"Well, obviously I can't be certain," she said. "I mean they never actually told me anything directly."

"But?" Lyons prompted gently.

"But yes," she replied. "Yes, I think they're probably planning some sort of military seizure of this government."

It was just after two o'clock in the morning. Although Harwood's safehouse lay only eighteen miles across the Potomac from Washington, it felt no less remote than that lodge where the generals had met. The surrounding roads, poorly paved and unlit, were deserted. The hills, too, were very quiet except for the occasional bark of a dog.

In contrast to the lodge, however, the senator had finally managed to instill a sense of warmth to this house. In addition to the portraits of the founding fathers, for example, he had hung a few Impressionist prints. He had also removed the plastic covering from the lamp shades and the heavy curtains from the windows.

"Maybe it's time to talk about tactics," Harwood said when Molly had grown quiet again. "Maybe it's time to get down to brass tacks and decide whether or not we tell the President."

But Severson, who sipped at a large Scotch, merely smiled. "Frankly, I don't really think the President's going to be much help at this point, John. In fact, once he realizes that he can't just pick up the phone and call in a strike, I think he's going to panic."

"Well, he's got to be told sooner or later."

"Agreed, but not until we've worked out the military solution."

At which point an exhausted Molly went upstairs to bed and Blancanales was called in from the next room to join Lyons, Schwarz, Severson and the senator.

"Basically what we're looking at is a hard terror strike and then a quick power grab," Severson began. "Now, I can't be certain exactly what they've got planned, but I think I've got a pretty fair idea as to the parameters."

"And those are?" Harwood asked.

Severson withdrew a notebook, not unlike the one that Rambling Ray Doyle had withdrawn earlier that evening. "First," he began, "I think we've got to assume that their primary goal will be to create widespread panic in and around at least four major metropolitan areas."

"To what end?" Harwood asked.

"In a word," Severson replied, "it will provide the excuse to put this nation under martial law."

Severson laid the notebook on the nineteenth-century tea chest that passed for a coffee table. He then picked up two pewter cups, a beaten brass ashtray and a handful of matchsticks from a lacquered box. These objects were also placed on the chest and would serve as his instructional aids.

"I've done some checking," he began, "and I think I've come up with a pretty reliable scenario." Then sliding one of the cups into the center of the table, he said, "Are you familiar with the L.I.W. report?"

Harwood glanced at Lyons and Blancanales, but neither man offered any help. "L.I.W. report?"

"Low Intensity Warfare," Severson continued. "It's the latest buzz word in the Pentagon and it basically refers to any brushfire conflict involving counterinsurgency or anti-terrorist forces. Up until recently, however, the term was usually applied to Third World action: Nicaragua, Sri Lanka, El Salvador, Africa. Then about eighteen months ago, the Pentagon released their domestic L.I.W. assessment and all of a sudden people started rethinking the whole concept in terms of the big city."

Severson picked up a second pewter cup and placed it in the center of the table. "Let's say this is Washington," he said. Then placing a couple of matchsticks beside the cup, he added, "And let's say these are the extremely high voltage lines. Now, ever since the big New York power blackout of '77, a lot's been done to protect the power grids from massive chain reaction failures. But that doesn't mean you still can't cut a city's power supply by hitting the EHV transformers. And once you've done that, you're talking wide-eyed panic . . . particularly when coupled with some of the other little tricks they might have up their sleeve."

"What kind of tricks?" Harwood asked, his gaze now fixed on the tea chest.

Severson dropped another match on the chest. "Gas Lines. Seventy-one percent of this nation's domestic natural gas is produced in Texas and Louisiana. You cut the transportation lines, or feed in a troublesome substance, and you're talking real trouble."

"And by a troublesome substance you mean?"

"Hydrogen cyanide," Lyons said.

Harwood rose from his chair, and limped to the window. Although fully recovered from his injuries, he occasionally favored his right leg and in moments of extreme stress, he tended to have problems with his back.

"But how can you be certain?" he asked softly. "I mean how do you know for certain that's going to be their game plan?"

Severson shook his head. "We're not certain, but all the indicators are there."

"For example," Lyons added, "one of the game boards out at the Wolf's Tooth includes an exact model of the capital and it's outlying power stations. Now, it's always possible that they're merely planning *defensive* actions, but I don't think so. I think they're planning to throw this nation into chaos, and then use that chaos as an excuse to seize power."

"And the Senate?" Harwood asked. "The Congress?"

"According to the scenario outlined in the Capital Defense Game," Severson replied, "both legislative bodies are to be quickly eliminated."

Harwood stepped away from the window, sank into a low settee and ran a weary hand across his forehead. "Why?" he whispered. "Why?"

Severson shrugged. "Like I told you, it's probably just a consequence of the circumstances. You keep feeding a military until it reaches the size of the one we've got and sooner or later they're going to start biting the hand that fed them. They can't help it. It's their nature. From their viewpoint this country has been going down the tubes for a long time— drugs, crime, financial ruin. The civilians can't solve it, not even the radical right. So maybe it's time to give the military a chance . . . or at least that's the way they see it."

"So what do we do to fight them?" Harwood asked after another lengthy silence. "I mean, how do you enlist an army to fight your own Army?"

"We use what we got," Lyons replied. "We use whatever we can dig up from the peripheral ranks and then we hit them on their own ground where they're not expecting it."

"We also might want to give them a little taste of what they've got planned for us," Blancanales added.

At which point, Schwarz, who had more or less been dozing again by the fire, opened his eyes and grinned.

IT WAS JUST AFTER FOUR O'CLOCK in the morning when the meeting finally ended. Although painfully exhausted after the night flight in from Albuquerque, Lyons insisted on accompanying Severson out along the deer path to the circle of pines where he had left his rented Le Baron. Despite the chill the air felt good, and the sky was bright with stars.

"I think we're going to have to assume that they may escalate their timetable," Lyons said as they followed the rutted path deeper into the shadow of the pines.

"We also have to assume that they're not going to forget about you and the girl," Severson added.

Lyons took a long, slow breath of damp air, then shook his head and briefly shut his eyes. "Yeah, well I don't think we've got time to worry about that right now," he said. "Right now, we've got to start recruiting."

Severson nodded, but then also shook his head. "It's not going to be easy. Even if we go to the outlying commands, we'll still be facing the same basic problem that always arises sooner or later in situations like this: who do we trust? How will we know for certain that we're not talking to a commander who isn't already part of the plot?"

"We won't," Lyons breathed. "Unfortunately, we won't."

THE COTTAGE WAS DARK and silent when Lyons returned. Although the sound of the lifting latch may have disturbed Blancanales, the others were apparently asleep. Yet as Lyons continued up the staircase in search of a spare bed or couch, he heard a faint whisper calling his name from the black-ness.

"Carl? Carl, is that you?"

He leaned against the door, nodded, then realized that Molly probably still couldn't actually see him. "Yeah," he said quietly. "It's me."

She was kneeling on the bed, wearing only a shirt that she had borrowed from the senator and a silver bangle around her left wrist. Her hair, recently washed, hung in loose blond curls across her eyes. A thin line of moonlight from the window illuminated her slender thighs.

"Do you need a place to sleep?" she asked softly. Then shrugging with a shy smile she continued, "I mean I wouldn't mind if you wanted to...well, you know, stay here for a while."

He returned her smile, but finally shook his head. "Maybe some other time," he said.

"Sure." She sighed. "Maybe some other time."

But before he could actually turn to leave, she suddenly whispered his name again.

"Carl, please wait. *Please.*"

Then although he told her that he would only stay for a while, it was well past dawn before he finally managed to pry himself from her arms.

18

Treason, Severson concluded, is quite often simply a matter of habit. The American soldier, who empties a magazine into a crowd of civilians, may not be conscious that he is violating the law. Indeed, he may simply be doing what he was trained to do: follow orders. Given this conclusion, Severson decided that he would ultimately have to raise his counterforce from outside the regular chains of command—from what is sometimes called the Shadow World and generally includes a whole array of mercenaries, psycho killers and misfit adventurers.

It was Thursday when Severson and Lyons actually began the delicate task of recruitment. They began with what Severson called the oblique approach, placing four or five seemingly casual telephone calls to old friends from the secret world, then finally arranging a meeting with a certain Colonel Stewart Folly whom he had known for at least twenty years. Folly then telephoned a Major Jack Horton from the Defense Intelligence Agency, who in turn telephoned a certain Colonel York T. Black from the CIA's Operations Directorate. Concurrently, Lyons also made four or five telephone calls to various soldiers he had fought with through the years, but ultimately it all led back to the notorious Colonel Black.

York Thomas Black was one of a number of irregulars who had knocked around in foreign wars under dubious authority from the White House. In certain respects, he was not unlike Jennings Vaughan and the others who had been recruited on the sly to help with the formation of the Domestic Counterinsurgency Program. Yet, by the same token, he was not without ethical standards. He had refused, for example, to fight with the Contras on the grounds that much of their support was financed by the sale of cocaine. Similarly he had refused to fight with the Chinese nationalists in Burma, because virtually all of their support was heroin based. Yet when the North Vietnamese began to slaughter the Cambodian peasants, he immediately moved into the jungle to help with the resistance. He'd fought the Cubans in Africa, and had spent nearly twenty months in Afghanistan, fighting with the Mujahedeen rebels. Recently, however, he was generally known to have been on everyone's shit list for having blown the whistle on a crooked defense contractor—he'd also beaten him to a pulp for good measure.

Physically, Black was a beefy man, with steel gray hair and gray-green eyes. Since Lyons had seen him last, a fragment of Soviet shrapnel had taken off the tip of his left index finger and left a pencil-line scar along his jaw. Otherwise, however, the man hadn't changed. There was the same catlike elegance, the same slow and thoughtful speech pattern, the same probing intellect and wry sense of humor.

It was late Wednesday when Lyons and Severson met with Black. After catching an afternoon shuttle to Tampa, they rented yet another Honda and crossed the causeway into Clearwater. There they found Black waiting in a rented condominium high above the bay. It was raining but warm. Black wore a wrinkled white tropical suit but no shoes. On the table was a fifth of tequila, a ceramic bowl of salt and another of sliced limes.

"So, Lyle," Black smiled as his guests entered the room, "what crisis has brought you to my little netherworld?" Then finally rising, he extended his hand to Lyons, "You look well, Carl. Indeed one might say that you even look alive."

In accordance with Black's tastes the room reflected an oddly exotic elegance, with unpainted brick, potted palms and hardwood floors. Among the etchings on the walls, were two numbered Picassos and what may have been a genuine Degas. There was also a shark's jaw above the fireplace and an assortment of pre-Colombian artifacts.

"We've got a job for you," Severson began. "Interested?"

Black smiled again, toying with an ebony cigarette holder.

"It's not what you think," Lyons said. "It's not what you think at all."

But again Black merely smiled. "I'm afraid that I already have a job—clearly defined and far away. Besides, I've been blackballed . . . or haven't you heard?"

Severson poured a shot of tequila, then sprinkled a little salt between his thumb and forefinger. "It's not precisely an official assignment," he said. "In fact you might even call it below the line."

"They say that I'm particularly on the outs with the Bush league," Black added. "Presumably because I had the affront to imply that the President may not have told the whole truth regarding his rodeo with the cocaine cowboys."

"Yeah, well this has nothing to do with that," Lyons replied. "This is domestic."

"All the more reason why I'm most probably not the sort of man you're looking for," Black countered.

"On the contrary," Severson put in. "I think you're exactly the sort of man we're looking for." Then withdrawing a copy of the Game Report and tossing it to the glass-topped coffee table, he sat back and waited.

In all Black spent nearly fifteen minutes examining the report...hunched in his chair, toying with a loose strand of hair and remaining entirely silent. When he had finished he moved to the far end of the room overlooking an expansive display of boats bobbing in the gray sea.

"I seem to recall that it was Eisenhower who first spoke out against the dangers of that so-called military-industrial complex," Black said at last. "In his farewell speech, I believe. 'We must guard against the acquisition of unwarranted influences, whether sought or unsought by the military-industrial complex. The potential for the disastrous rise of misplaced power exists and will persist.' Or something like that."

"Well, it happens to have gone a lot further than that," Severson replied from across the room. "In fact, it happens to have gone well past any normal nightmare."

"So then go to Congress. Go to the Senate. Call the *Washington Post*, the *New York Times*, and get your friend Harwood to blow the whistle on Ted Koppel's show."

"It's too late for all that," Lyons said. "It's too late for anything but affirmative action."

Black turned from the window, suddenly looking more like a tropical recluse than ever, with dark circles beneath his eyes and beads of perspiration across his forehead. "Does the President know?" he finally asked.

"Not yet," Severson replied.

"What about the Secret Service?"

"No."

"Well, shit, what have you been doing?"

"Figuring out a way to contact someone like you," Lyons said.

Black smiled, but then shook his head again. "Look, I've only got about a hundred men," he finally said.

"A hundred should just about do it," Lyons replied.

"Against the entire United States Army? That's rich. That's very rich. Besides, my men are misfits, hopeless misfits from the worst alleys of the secret world."

"What's their current status?" Lyons asked.

Black shrugged. "Officially, they're in training as a peacekeeping unit to be stationed in Beirut. Unofficially, we're probably all bound for some place like Angola, where we can kill and be killed without raising too much attention."

"And who was the program director?" Severson asked, pouring another shot of tequila.

Black shrugged again, this time with a thin smile. "Dickie Sax, but since the election I rather think we've more or less been forgotten."

"But essentially you're battle ready?"

Black cocked his head to the side with a smirk. "Not to go up against the kind of might that Rambling Ray Doyle will throw at us. I mean once you start talking about Rambling Ray and Arthur Matoon Clancy, you're talking about all sorts of unpleasant variables. You're talking tank battalions, gunships and fleets of those nasty little Cobras... and that's just the conventional stuff."

"Yes, well, we're not exactly expecting you to meet them head-on," Severson said.

"Then what?"

"Think of it as a dental operation. We'll supply the pliers. You supply the muscle, and together we'll pull out that damn Wolf's Tooth."

"And if those jaws happen to close before we've completed the job?"

"Then we'll all be missing a finger or two," Lyons smiled.

THEY ADJOURNED TO THE BEACH, to a long stretch of sandy shore between a lighthouse and a crumbling wharf. Although the rain had stopped, the fog had moved in with the wind. There were also gulls above, dozens of them circling and crying.

"I'm not sure what else to tell you," Severson said as they moved along the cold sand. "I mean there's really nothing much riding on this except perhaps the Constitution, the Bill of Rights and the basic fabric of this nation's democracy."

"Why don't you just tell me the plan?" Black replied. "Why don't you just tell me how you expect to knock out Ray Doyle with a hundred maniacs?"

Lyons picked up a piece of driftwood, and proceeded to draw a circle in the sand. "Let's say this is the Wolf's Tooth compound," he said. "Company strength, and armed to the teeth."

"I like it already," Black smirked.

"But the fact of the matter is," Lyons continued, "they're not a defensive body. They're offensive . . . strictly offensive."

"And thus vulnerable to a quick kick in the teeth?" Black smiled. "Is that your point?"

Lyons nodded, drawing a second circle in the sand. "Way I figure it, we should probably hit them here along the eastern perimeter, then move in real quick before they get a chance to launch their choppers."

"What if they call them in from the Kirtland base nearby?"

"Well, that's pretty much the whole point, isn't it? The Wolf's Tooth unit is the advance guard. Once the word gets around that we've taken them out, it's the same as lopping off the monster's head. The rest of the conspirators should run for the hills."

"And what if you're wrong? What if they simply throw in one of the other Special Forces groups. The SEALs, for example. What if they throw in the SEALs?"

"Then we've got a problem," Severson said. "But in all honesty I tend to think that Carl is right. If we can take out the Wolf's Tooth unit, the rest of the conspiracy will collapse."

Black also picked up a slender piece of driftwood, then also began drawing circles in the sand. But suddenly rising to his feet again, he tossed the stick away and turned to face the water.

"My boys are stationed about fifteen miles from here," he said. "Filthy little place on the edge of the swamp. Isn't even on the map. But if you can get us out of there, we can probably arrange our own transport into the sector."

"What about equipment?" Lyons asked.

"Equipment we've got. Equipment isn't the problem."

"How about the brief?" Severson asked. "I mean what do you suggest your men be told?"

Black shrugged. "Well, seeing as how they're going to be killing American soldiers, I suggest that we tell them the truth."

19

The President took the news of a possible military coup badly. Although much of his campaign had been devoted to erasing his "wimp" image, Harwood had hardly finished speaking before the man began to panic. To begin with he went white as a sheet while tiny geysers of perspiration erupted on his forehead. Sheer terror flashed in his eyes.

"What about the Coast Guard?" he finally managed to ask.

"The Coast Guard, Mr. President?" Harwood replied.

"That's right, the Coast Guard. Surely the Coast Guard can't be involved in this."

Harwood eased his gaze past the President's desk to the view of the frozen garden through the windows of the Oval Office. Although a fire burned in the massive grate and the temperature in the room couldn't have been much below seventy degrees, there was a distinctly unnatural chill in the air.

"No, Mr. President," Harwood said at last, "I don't imagine that the Coast Guard would be involved."

"Then that's the answer. We'll hit him with the Coast Guard. Maybe throw in the National Guard for good measure."

Harwood ran a hand across his mouth and glanced back to the corridor where the President's National Security Adviser waited in the wings. Also waiting to be briefed were two members of the Secret Service and the Secretary of State. Beyond that, however, Harwood had insisted that no one be told…at least not yet, not while Able Team was still marshalling their response.

"Frankly, Mr. President, I have the feeling that the Coast Guard may not be the answer."

"All right, then you tell me," the President snapped back. "Go on, tell me what we do about this!"

"At the moment, sir, nothing."

"Nothing? You inform me that my military is about to seize control of this government and then suggest that I do nothing?"

"Until we receive the word from Severson's team, yes."

"And then what?"

"Then I would suggest that you send a couple of Secret Service agents to round up your generals and proceed from there."

The President shook his head and whispered unintelligibly. Then slightly louder, he said, "Why? After all I've done for those bastards … why this?"

Harwood shrugged. "Mr. President, you know what they say: a little power corrupts a little, a lot of power corrupts even more."

"But I've given them everything they want!"

"And like everyone else, they want more."

AT PRECISELY THE SAME TIME that Harwood was visiting the President, Severson was briefing the only other essential player in his game plan: Deputy Director of Counterintelligence, Humphrey Knoll. Like Severson, Knoll was old school: suave, soft-spoken and politically elusive. A round little man with thinning hair and an oddly childish face, Knoll was generally thought of as the quintessential counterspy—a truly paranoid man, with an almost infinite capacity for suspicion. Indeed, it was commonly said that the only person Humphrey Knoll trusted was his mother...assuming, of course, that the woman who supposedly bore him *was* in fact his mother.

Given the air of suspicion, not to mention the subject of their talk, Severson and Knoll met outside the CIA complex in what is sometimes called the Dulles glade. Like the grounds outside the Oval Office, the landscape here was suspended between the state of freezing and thawing. The rose stalks were bare. The oaks were leafless. The lawns were shrouded with frost.

"Technically, I suppose it's quite an interesting problem," Knoll remarked casually after hearing Severson's brief. "How does one protect the Constitution against those very forces designed to protect it in the first place? Really quite interesting."

"Unfortunately it's not just an intellectual exercise," Severson replied. "Unfortunately this is for real."

Knoll eased his little body onto one of the icy benches that lined the edge of the glade, and lit a cigarette.

"I don't suppose you've thought about informing the FBI?"

Severson shrugged. "What for? So they can contact Rambling Ray and cut themselves in on the deal?"

"How about the Secret Service?"

"Well, in as much as we may need a little local muscle, yes. But I hardly think they'd be a match for Doyle's Special Forces team. Anyway, I don't think we're in a position to play it defensively."

"Then what's the plan?"

Severson also sank to the bench. "We're going to try and shoot the lead dog," he said. Then briefly smiling, "Or should I say the lead wolf?"

Knoll tossed away his cigarette, and jammed his hands a little deeper into the pockets of his trench coat. "I suppose you realize that if you fail, they'll probably put your head on a pike."

Severson shrugged again. "If I fail, we'll all be on the pike," he said, "but frankly I'm not planning on failing...not so long as I can maintain the element of surprise."

"And that's dependent upon me?" Knoll asked.

Severson smiled again, but only for a moment. "I'd like to borrow a few of your people," he said at last.

"Borrow, Lyle?"

"Just for a night or two."

As if suddenly growing very nervous, Knoll rose to his feet and began to pace across the frozen grass. His voice, however, was still controlled.

"You're asking for a lot, Lyle."

"I'm asking you to help save this nation from fascism, Humph. I'm asking you to give me four or five men, so that I can keep the generals on ice while my team knocks out the Wolf's Tooth."

"And by keeping them on ice you mean...?"

"I mean keeping them under house arrest."

"At gunpoint?"

"If necessary."

"For how long?"

"Ten hours, maybe twelve."

"What if something goes wrong? What if someone hits the panic button, or even—God forbid—calls the cops?"

"If you give me the right sort of men, I think that kind of unpleasantness can be avoided."

Severson also rose to his feet and started pacing with his eyes fixed on the frozen ground. "Look, if anything goes wrong," he said, "I'll testify that you didn't even know about it. I'll testify that I simply pulled rank and took your men without asking."

Knoll drew to a stop, gazing dully around him at the blackened boughs and iced leaves. "Well, I'll tell you, Lyle, I rather suspect that if anything goes wrong you're not going to have a chance to testify. They're simply going to put you up against a wall and shoot you."

EVEN MOLLY MEEKIN had been permitted to give a briefing on that last cold morning before the Wolf's Tooth counterstrike. In order to conduct this briefing she had been instructed to borrow one of the rented Fords and drive at least twenty miles to a pay phone. She had also been instructed not to talk more than three minutes and not to give even the slightest clue as to the gravity of her situation.

Yet when she finally dialed the number and heard her mother's watery hello, it was all she could do to keep from breaking down again.

"Mom?"

"Molly? Molly, where are you?"

"Mom, I just want to tell you that I'm all right."

"Molly, your father and I have been worried sick about you."

"I understand, Mom, but I won't be away much longer."

"But where have you been? What have you been doing?"

"I can't tell you that right now. All I can say is that I'm all right, and I love you both very much."

"But, how do we—"

"I've got to go, Mom."

"Molly, are you sure everything's...I mean you don't sound like—"

"Please, Mom, just trust me. Everything's fine."

By the time she replaced the receiver, however, her hands were shaking and her face was wet with tears.

20

It was raining when Captain Black's strike force rendez-voused with Able Team at an isolated landing strip below the mesa. It was a thin but cold rain made even colder with the wind, but the temperature would keep the sentries inside and the wind would play hell with the choppers.

Lyons and company saw very little when they first reached the landing strip: a thirty-year-old AC-47 parked at the edge of the tarmac, three or four unattended crates below the left wing, the black badlands beyond. Then by degrees, Black's team emerged from the shadows of sandstone and sage: ninety-five silent soldiers in jeans, unpolished GI boots, black field jackets and black Navy watch caps. On the right shoulder of each jacket was stitched an American flag, but otherwise they were entirely unidentifiable, a ghost team.

Carl Lyons was essentially pleased with the men that made up Black's team. For the most part, they were originally from the same stock as the Wolf's Tooth unit. Twenty or thirty of them had been selected from the 10th Special Forces group at Fort Devon. Another twenty or so had been sifted out of 5th and 7th group in the south. Then there were those who had been more or less poached from the regular Army, after demonstrating an unusual ferocity. Although less than a dozen were old enough to have seen extended action in Vietnam, nearly all had seen combat at one point or another: some in Grenada, some in El Salvador, some in the Middle East.

Although Lyons had prepared a brief speech en route from Virginia, in the end he simply read a letter from the President. But given the fact that most of Black's men were basically rebels who had never respected the Pentagon's power structure to begin with, it really didn't matter what the President said. They knew that if they failed, Rambling Ray Doyle and Arthur Matoon Clancy would probably end up running the nation and that would be an unacceptable situation.

Finally, and almost as an afterthought, there was also a word or two about tactics. Essentially, Lyons told the ranks of men, the success of their mission was wholly dependent upon surprise. For that reason the approach would have to be entirely silent. Weapons were to be locked. Clips were to be taped. Small arms were to be secured to the webbing. As a further precaution, Lyons ordered the point men to carry silent weapons: knives, wire and IDG M-36 sniper systems, with integral flash suppressors and muzzle brakes. The heavier weapons—the H&K MP-5 9 mm parabellums, the HK-21 light machine guns and the M-203 grenade launchers would come later.

Naturally there were questions about tanks, specifically the new Abrams M-1, supposedly mounted with stabilized autocannon for a ninety percent first-hit probability. Yet given that the team would be packing only light antitank weapons in collapsible firing tubes, Lyons did not really have an answer.

In closing, the Able Team warrior also felt obliged to at least mention the emotional side of things. He said that it was very likely that at one point or another they would find themselves facing men they had known from Fort Devon or one of the other Special Forces groups. "Maybe it will be someone who once gave you a smoke," he said, "someone who once bought you a beer, or covered your ass on the combat course. It might even be someone you considered a real buddy, somebody you would have died for fifteen months ago. But if you let any of those emotions block your response, even for a split second, you're going to be dead and no one will thank you for it. Understood?"

Then came the handshakes, the mumbled words of good luck and the last nervous glances over the shoulder. Although they moved fairly quickly at first, the muddy slopes and jagged ravines eventually slowed them to a crawl. Closer to the edge of the mesa, there were also problems with loose sandstone, swollen streams and frost.

IT WAS EXACTLY eleven o'clock when Colonel Black's forward team sighted the first two Wolf's Tooth sentries. The sighting was made with a hand-held image intensifier, then word of it was immediately passed back to Schwarz, Blancanales and Lyons. The sentries, apparently armed with an M-60 belt-fed machine gun and M-79 grenade launchers, were stationed in a bunker that had been constructed just inside the wire. Although apparently awake and alert, they only occasionally swept the landscape with their own night-vision systems.

"I'm open to anything," Black said. "You want me to send a couple of guys through the wire? I'll tell them to start stripping down. You want to try to pop them from here? I'll break out the launchers. I'm open to anything at all."

"What about just sitting tight and letting Blancanales and me take them out on a prowl?" Lyons replied.

Black glanced over his shoulder at the kneeling form of Blancanales, then along the dark ranks of his own men. "You know, I happen to have guys who specialize in that sort of thing," he said at last. "In fact, I got guys who live for it."

"Yeah, I'm sure you do," Lyons said, "but I kind of think that I'd rather test the water myself."

THEY WERE CROUCHED in a shallow ravine seventy-five yards in from the mesa cliffs. The ground ahead was flat and bare, except for clusters of cactus, sage and Joshua. Although there were no lights along the compound's perimeter, the towers were cleanly etched against the angry sky, the bunkers were visible against the horizon. There was also the outline of something that Lyons hadn't noticed before: some sort of multiple role combat vehicle, mounted with what looked like a 25 mm gun. The moment Lyons and Blancanales started moving out, however, all they focused on were the sentries.

The wind-blown shadows from sage and cactus covered their approach for the first eighty yards. For the next thirty yards they were able to advance in the relative safety of a narrow streambed. The last forty yards, however, were virtually barren.

"If they spot us," Lyons whispered, "then you might as well just open up with everything you got. You understand what I'm saying? If they spot us, we're not going to have a whole lot of choices left."

Blancanales nodded, inching his gaze above a low tangle of sage to the hunched outline of a sentry behind the sandbags. Although the H&K MP-5 had long been a favored weapon of the Special Forces groups, it was not particularly suited for the kind of distance that now faced Blancanales. He was also a little worried about the sighting, which had been intentionally adjusted for close-quarter work.

They took the last twenty yards at a crawl. Although the rain had eased to a drizzle, the wind continued to sing through the wire and whistle through the mounds of sage. When they finally reached the chain link fence, they paused again . . . waiting, listening, virtually becoming just another innocuous shadow. Then finally withdrawing a pair of wire cutters, Lyons rolled on his back and proceeded to open a hole in the fence.

Once beyond the wire, they again moved at a slow crawl. Although their vision of the sentries was obscured by the sandbags, the voices were faintly audible. One of them was saying something about a girl named Gina, while the other laughed in response. There was also the smell of cigarettes and coffee, and what sounded like a selector switch being rapidly switched from fully automatic to semiautomatic over and over again.

"How you want to play it?" Blancanales whispered from the blackness of the drainage ditch.

Lyons discarded his MP-5 and withdrew an Applegate-Gaibairn boot knife, and his modified .45 auto. "Let me see if I can't move in behind them and take them the easy way."

Blancanales peered around the sandbags for another quick glimpse at the silhouettes. "What if they don't want to play?"

"Then pop them both," Lyons said.

Approximately fifty feet lay between the drainage ditch and the bunker—fifty feet of cold, flat ground. Given the lay of the shadows and direction of the wind, however, Lyons was fairly confident that he would not be detected. He moved at a slow crawl, vaguely resembling some sort of predatory lizard. As he drew closer, he caught the scent of Old Spice and actually heard the pop of chewing gum.

The sentries were younger than Lyons had imagined. The taller of the two, a slender blond kid from either Kentucky or West Virginia, couldn't have been much older than twenty-two or twenty-three. The other, the dark and stocky kid with a Brooklyn accent, was probably no more than twenty-five. They were probably picked up from one of the Airborne teams, Lyons thought, initially selected because they had scored well on the jump-dodge-run course. Then obviously possessing one or more special skills, they were finally given at least a Grade Five on their second enlistment tests.

But the real test, Lyons thought grimly as he closed the last four feet, was about to come right now....

He hesitated only a second or two before finally making his move. Then rising from the shadows below the lip of the bunker, he snaked out his left arm, coiled it around the younger kid's neck and extended his .45 to the older kid.

"Easy," he hissed. "Real easy."

But although the younger one froze immediately, his buddy had already grabbed an M-16.

Another two or three entirely motionless seconds passed, as Lyons and the soldier from Brooklyn simply looked at one another, and the soldier from the south continued to shiver in Lyons's grip.

"It doesn't have to play this way," Lyons whispered. "You can just put down that weapon and walk away from it."

"Listen to him, Olie," the kid from Virginia whispered. "Listen to the man."

But Olie simply continued to stare—his gaze fixed on the .45 auto, while his own weapon remained fixed on Lyons's face.

"Can't do it, man," he finally replied. "Just can't do it."

Then finally letting his lips spread into an oddly dreamy smile, he began to squeeze the trigger.

Lyons fired from a half crouch. He fired as much out of instinct as anything else. Then as the stocky kid's head exploded and the slender kid started to scream, he fired again.

Blood and fragments of brain sprayed across the bunker, splattering into the slender kid's face. But by this time the kid had managed to twist out of Lyons's grip and reaching for his own side arm, he spun around. Lyons shouted, "It's not worth it, soldier!" But having already started to move, the boy couldn't stop himself now.

Lyons squeezed off two shots as the boy brought his own .45 into play. The first slug sent the boy tumbling back into the body of his buddy, while the second tore a fist-size hole in the kid's chest. Then, although both bodies continued to twitch for another two or three seconds, it was obvious that both sentries were dead.

"It was a judgment call," Blancanales said when he finally joined Lyons in the bunker. "You played it all the way to line, then you had to make a judgment call."

Lyons nodded, but still said nothing: eyes fixed on the faces of the soldiers, his .45 still dangling from his limp right arm.

"There's no mileage in this," Lyons said with a disgusted frown. "You know what I'm talking about? There's just no mileage in this."

Blancanales sank to a knee, and picked up the Starlite scope. Although the wind was still blowing hard form the northeast, he was nonetheless concerned that the shots had been heard in the tower.

"Look," he finally said, "you gave them both as much slack as you could. They knew what was happening, and they decided to disregard it."

"You think so, huh?" Lyons smirked. "You really think so? Well, let me tell you something, Pol, these kids weren't playing government takeover. They were just doing what they were supposed to be doing: following orders. They didn't know nothing about politics. All they knew is what they were told to know, and now they're dead for it."

"Yeah, so what's the point?"

"The point is," Lyons said, "they were American soldiers. You understand what I'm saying? These kids were *American* soldiers."

21

Corporal Jorge Pablo Sanchez braced his wiry body against the watch tower railing and scanned the far perimeter.

"You hear anything?" he asked. "Hey, gringo, you hear anything?" he repeated when he received no reply from Corporal Shrieve.

Shrieve put down his copy of *Playboy*, but didn't rise to his feet. "No, I didn't hear nothing."

Although Sanchez and Shrieve were not exactly friends, they had known one another for more than four years. They had both been to Grenada and Beirut, and had even enjoyed some R&R together in New Orleans.

"Well, I heard something, man," Sanchez said after another long silence. "I don't know what, but I definitely heard something moving around down there."

Shrieve finally rose to his feet, and picked up the Starlite scope. Yet after scanning the perimeter as far as the drainage ditch, he switched off the power and smirked, "There ain't nothing out there but a bunch of tumbleweeds... tumbleweeds and rats."

But Sanchez still couldn't seem to tear his eyes off the landscape below...the forbidding expanse of sand and sage, the dim outline of chain link and the equally dim outline of the Joshua trees. Then finally turning his gaze still farther afield, he caught a glimpse of at least a dozen shadows scrambling out of the bunker.

"Hey, Shrieve," he whispered. "Hey, maybe you'd better take a look at this."

"Take a look at what?" Shrieve sighed, also scanning the ground again. "I don't see nothing."

"Well, I'm telling you I saw something, man. You hear me, man? I'm telling you there's *definitely* something out there."

Shrieve reached for a red telephone that connected the tower to central security. Before he actually lifted the receiver, however, he turned to Sanchez again. "If this turns out to be a false alarm, man, you're taking the heat. That understood? You bring out the sergeant for nothing, and you're taking the heat."

"Look, just make the call," Sanchez said. "Okay? Just make the call."

Yet when Shrieve finally picked up the receiver, all he heard was the wind.

"It's dead," Shrieve said. The blood slowly drained from his face and the receiver slipped out of his hand as he repeated himself, "It's dead."

GADGETS SCHWARZ slipped the wire cutters into his belt, and eased himself back onto the main support strut below the sentries. Although he was still precariously balanced forty feet above the cold ground, he slowly lifted an arm to signal the others below.

"That's it," Lyons whispered to Black. "He's got them isolated."

Black flipped the selector switch down to three-burst mode and glanced back to the ill-defined faces of his advance team. Behind the advance team, at least another forty or fifty hunched forms lay among the shadows.

"So how do you want to play it?" Black replied. "You want to try to take them up close, or what?"

"Yeah," Lyons breathed. "I want to take them up close."

He moved off in a half crouch, running like some predatory insect into the deeper shadows below the tower. Behind him, like the perfectly synchronized legs of a scorpion, Black led six more men into the darkness. They began the long and slow climb up the ladder. When they reached the halfway point where Schwarz perched on a cross beam, Lyons called another brief halt.

But having obviously heard or sensed something, the guards were also silent.

"HAND ME THE SPOTLIGHT," Shrieve whispered. "Hand me the spotlight, and we'll nail them right to the wire."

But Sanchez shook his head. "You turn on that light, man, and they'll pick us off like flies."

They had crouched down on the floor of the observation booth. Despite the chill, they were both sweating profusely and Shrieve couldn't seem to keep his hands from shaking.

"All right, then what's your idea?" he asked. "Huh, spic? What's your idea?"

Sanchez picked up his MP-5, eased back the bolt to insert a 9 mm bullet in the chamber, and slid over to the door of the booth. "My idea," he said softly, "is to get out of this thing in one piece. That's my idea."

There were echoes of what may have been a rubber-soled shoe on the ladder, then possibly the noise of a zipper sliding across one of the support beams. Finally Sanchez even heard what may have been the sound of an automatic being cocked.

"They're close," he whispered. "They're real close."

But it wasn't until he actually peered through the door of the observation booth and caught a quick glimpse of something rising above the edge of the platform that he finally opened up.

LYONS SWUNG FROM THE platform as a spray of 9 mm rounds rang off the steel around him. On the ladder below at least three members of Black's forward team had cocked their weapons, while Black had withdrawn a grenade. But just as suddenly it was quiet again, with only the wind singing through the chain link.

"You up there!" Lyons called out in a harsh whisper. "We are acting under Presidential orders. Abandon your weapons and come down."

More silence, then possibly the double click of a magazine sliding into place.

"I repeat, we are acting under Presidential orders. Now, put away your weapons and climb down."

A third and fourth click of what may have been an M-60.

"It ain't going to happen," Black whispered. "It just ain't going to happen."

But even as Lyons eased off the safety and withdrew a stun grenade, there was suddenly the clatter of a dropping weapon and a distinctly Hispanic voice saying, "Well, suck this shit, man. I ain't going eat it for no political dispute. No way. I'm coming on down."

But although there may have been a second voice from above, a distinctly Southern voice explaining that the weapons had now been discarded, the words were lost in the sudden hiss of a Viper antitank missile snaking up from the blackness below.

Lyons found himself bombarded with at least five split-second impressions as the nine pound, unguided warhead exploded into the observation booth above. Initially, of course, he was mainly conscious of the blast, the deafening crack and the blinding light. The blast was quickly followed by screams, the harsh screams of the sentries as a rain of hot steel and liquified Plexiglas instantly shredded their flesh. Then he was conscious of the shouts from below, the strangled cries of men leaping from the ladder to avoid the shrapnel. And then there was the blood jetting out from the severed arm of a soldier hit on the support beam beside him.

"Incoming!" Black began screaming as a storm of bullets rang off the steel girders around them. "We got incoming!"

Lyons caught a quick glimpse of a sniper named Hooper, clinging to a support beam and wincing with the impact of four high-velocity slugs. Then shaking his head and mouthing a silent prayer, the sniper suddenly plunged out of sight.

There were more shots from the far ground, and Lyons heard Schwarz yelling, "They're over by the storage bins!"

In response, however, five more high-velocity slugs echoed off the tower's superstructure, sending two more members of Black's assault team plunging off the ladder.

But by this time, Lyons had also seen the muzzle-flash from the shadows of the storage bins, and dropping his selector switch to full automatic, he squeezed off at least half a magazine. Below him, eight or nine others were also directing their fire toward the shadows of the bins.

But it wasn't until Blancanales hefted an M-203 grenade launcher and squeezed off two shells that the silence finally rolled back into the compound.

"We've got about seven minutes," Lyons said. "Seven minutes and they'll be on us like a swarm of bees."

Black surveyed the landscape ahead, his wary eyes sweeping the broad unlit gravel between the shattered tower and the first rank of barracks. On the cold ground around him lay the bodies of five men: three of his own and the two sentries. Still clinging to the superstructure below the blasted observation booth were two more shrapnel riddled bodies from his advance team.

"So how do you want to meet them?" Black finally asked.

Lyons glanced back to the thirty or forty pairs of eyes watching from the shadows behind him.

"Head-on." He finally sighed. "We're just going to have to meet them head-on."

22

Corporal Harris and Sergeant Trask stood at mute attention and watched their colonel pace. Although the colonel's initial response to the news of an intrusion had been to smash his fist into the fiberboard wall, he had finally grown exceptionally calm: eyes fixed on the window, left hand toying with a Browning 9 mm, a slow smile breaking on his lips.

"So be it," he finally breathed, "so be it." Then turning again to face his men, "They want to play hard ball? So be it."

Although the grounds had briefly been alive with the wail of sirens, Stack had ordered the alarms shut off. He had also ordered that the spotlights be dimmed and the electrified fences shut down. "Because there's no reason to panic," he had said. "No reason in the world to panic."

He turned to the window again and eased back the plastic blinds. Although there were still occasional bursts of small arms fire from the rim of the mesa, the perimeter was mostly quiet now... except, of course, for that northern wind.

"What's the estimated count?" he asked.

Sergeant Trask exchanged another quick glance with Harris, then said, "Far as we can tell, sir, there are about eighty or a hundred of them."

"Armed with?"

"Mostly HKs and grenade launchers, but they're probably also carrying at least a couple of M-60s and some Vipers to hit the tanks."

"Any idea who *they* are?"

This time it was Harris who glanced at Trask. "Well, it's possible that they're from York Black's unit down south, sir," Harris said. "At least that would be my guess."

Stack cocked his head with a slight smirk. "York Black, huh? Well, that's nice. That's real nice."

"Either way, they are definitely hostile, sir," Trask added. "Definitely hostile."

Stack let the blinds slide back into place, then turned again to face his men. Although he had only been awakened fifteen minutes earlier, neither Trask nor Harris had ever seen the man more alive, more invigorated.

"Now listen to me," the colonel said, "I don't care how you do it, but I want them eliminated. Is that clear? I don't want them pushed back. I don't want them captured. I want them completely eliminated."

"Yes, sir," Trask replied. "Eliminated."

"And one more thing, gentlemen. I've got a sneaking suspicion that you boys are also going to be facing that so-called Able Team again. Now, I don't have to tell you that the last time you played tag with them your performance was less than acceptable. So how about this time you do it right? What do you say? How about you boys go out and get me some scalps this time."

"Yes, sir," Trask nodded.

"TELL ME ABOUT THEM," Black said softly. "I want to know how they move, how they think, how they rebound off the net."

He was crouched beside Lyons and Blancanales in the secondary drainage ditch that ran below the outer storage bins. Although the ground ahead was quiet again, the echo of the sirens seemed to hang in the air. Now and again there were also sounds of mechanized movement: jeeps, light-armored vehicles with 25 mm mounts, and possibly even one of the M-1 Abrams tanks.

Lyons took a deep breath of chilly air and lowered his Starlite scope. "Most likely they'll come in two waves," he said, "probably behind some of that armor. But what you got to watch out for, is the heavy metal thrust, that's how they're going to try and nail us."

There were more echoes of mechanized equipment, and what may have been the rumble of a half-track on asphalt. Then just as suddenly, it was quiet again.

"What do you say we sucker them in, and then hit 'em from the wings?"

Lyons looked at Blancanales, who also took a long, hard breath.

"Word is that those tanks were fitted with laminated armor," Blancanales said. "You try to punch a hole in one of those laminated Abrams with a LAW and we could find ourselves in real trouble."

"Then, we'll just have to get close," Lyons replied. "We'll just have to get real close."

"TELL THEM TO KEEP THEIR distance," Trask said softly. "They start bunching up and we're all dead."

Although Trask had not actually served in a combat situation since the fall of Saigon, he was amazed at how quickly it all came back to him: the tightening of nerves, the heightened awareness, the sweet stench of tank exhaust and the easy tread of two hundred boots…it couldn't have been more familiar. He glanced past Harris to the ragged line of advancing men. He lifted his hand-held Starlite scope to his eyes, and scanned the dark ground ahead. He caught a glimpse of what may have been something scampering between the storage bins, then motioned to the flanking fire teams . . . all so familiar.

Beyond the barracks lay three clustered structures where Trask had decided his enemy would be waiting: the two rows of storage bins and the immediate action drilling field. It had also vaguely crossed his mind that if Lyons and company were involved, there might be action from the night course, but he wasn't particularly concerned about that area . . . not with the Abrams covering his ass.

A lieutenant appeared, a rangy Texan named Weber with a pencil moustache. The man had also seen action in Vietnam, but it was obvious that he hadn't a clue how to fight an elusive enemy on his own ground.

"Sergeant, your people are flagging," the lieutenant said softly. "You understand what I'm saying? Your people are flagging."

Trask lifted an arm, and brought his column to a halt. "With all due respect, sir," Trask whispered, "we are advancing at what I deem to be a prudent rate."

"And in the meantime your enemy is making himself nice and comfy. Now, if you are too chicken shit to advance without tank support, I will be most happy to contribute it. But I want this column to pick up the pace and start pressing the advance. Is that clear?"

"Yes, sir, entirely clear."

Trask took another quick look through his Starlite scope, motioned his men forward at a slightly faster pace. When the lieutenant had returned to his own unit, however, Trask immediately slowed the pace again. After forty yards he motioned the covering fire team to take position behind a handball court. After fifty yards he ordered Harris to deploy the snipers. Finally crossing still another sixty yards of relatively open ground to the first rank of bins, he lifted an arm to bring the remaining column to a halt.

Then for a long time, at least eight or nine minutes, he simply continued to scan the ground ahead: the two hundred yards of gravel and sand, the humped shapes of sage and chaparral, the rectangular shapes of the storage bins and the plywood barriers on the obstacle course.

"You want to play hero, or you want to play it safe?" he finally whispered to Harris.

Harris eased himself up from the half-frozen gravel, and also gazed out into the suggestive darkness. Then suddenly recalling the echo of those quad 50s ringing out across the mesa, he said, "I think I'd rather play it safe...if it's all the same to you."

At which point Trask reached for the radio to call up the Abrams.

ORIGINALLY DEVELOPED as *the* infantry combat vehicle of the 1980s, the laminated armor on the M-1 Abrams was designed to resist virtually all standard antitank weapons. The vehicle was further designed to go from 0 to 20 mph in six seconds flat, with a maximum speed of 45 mph—no mean feat for a sixty-ton machine. However, from the onset the vehicle had been plagued with problems...not the least of them a propensity to throw its tracks.

"All you want to do is stop it," Black whispered. "All you want to do is pop the tread."

Blancanales eased up the Viper, released the safety and sighted along the firing tube. Although capable of hurling an explosive shell through sixteen inches of armor, the weapon had never proven particularly effective against the newer generation of laminated armor.

It was growing colder along the drainage ditch, with thin layers of ice across the pools of rainwater and frost on the concrete siding. Blancanales didn't much care for the angle, and if he failed to stop that Abrams, the 7.62 mm machine guns would probably cut them to shreds. But ultimately he couldn't argue with Lyons's basic strategy: hit them head-on.

Blancanales lowered the Viper for a last quick look at the broad field. In all he had counted about fifty advancing men behind the Abrams—Harris and Trask among them. Although he, too, had initially been unable to entirely forget that these were American soldiers he was facing, all such thought evaporated when he had finally picked up the Viper. There was an approaching tank, an approaching column, and nothing else ultimately mattered.

"Whenever you're ready," he heard Black whisper. "Whenever you're ready."

Then lifting the Viper again and slowly shifting the sights until he saw nothing except dark steel, Blancanales squeezed the trigger.

TRASK WAS LESS THAN twenty yards from the Abrams when the first shell hit. Although he had told himself that contact could come at any moment, he had never imagined that the enemy would be foolish enough to hit him with a frontal assault.

He couldn't hear—that was his first thought. The blast had popped his eardrums and left him temporarily deaf. Trask quickly realized that the flash had ruined his night vision and that the concussion had messed up his equilibrium. He also knew that the Abrams had blown a tread, and that his men were catching small arms fire.

"Move!" he screamed. "Move your asses," he repeated as he caught sight of a crumpling soldier to his left.

There were three rows of sandbags opposite the drainage ditch. They had originally been laid as a barrier against overflow—they now provided Trask's men with at least some cover against the spray of automatic fire. There were also a dozen men still safely crouched behind the Abrams, and fire teams behind the recreation facilities.

"Now what?" Harris asked from directly behind Trask's shoulder. Although he was bleeding slightly above the left eye and was still suffering from the blast, his principle concern still lay ahead...to the darkened storage bins and drainage ditch where three minutes earlier he had counted at least thirty flashing muzzles. But he couldn't seem to take his eyes off the bodies—the seven twisted shapes laying around the Abrams.

"So how about it, sir?" he whispered. "What do we do now?"

Trask slowly raised his head above the sandbags and once more scanned the ground. Although also concerned about the sudden silence, he was certain that his enemy was still out there in strength.

"Get on the horn, and tell them to open up wide with that one-twenty," he breathed. "Then call back to the lieutenant, and tell him to bring me another goddamn tank."

"Now what?" Lyons asked.

Following Black's lead he had moved back with Schwarz, Blancanales and two dozen others to a shallow ravine below the storage bins. Following the first three strikes from the Abrams 120 mm cannon, they had retreated even further into the windblown chaparral.

"It's classic heavy-metal thrust," Black said softly. "They're likely just going to come right through there with everything they got," he said, turning to Lyons and pointing to the outline of Quonset huts in the distance.

"So what are the choices?" Schwarz asked.

But before anyone could reply, another shell from the Abrams's 120 exploded on the low ground to their left.

"How about we play it from the fringes again?" Lyons said when the rolling concussion had faded. "How about we slip on past the forward team and hit them before they've got a chance to organize."

Black ran a hand across his face to brush the sand from his eyebrows. "They catch you before you're set, and you'll end up eating some bad shit," he said.

But by this time there were already echoes of at least two more Abrams rumbling up from the rear, while the crippled tank in the foreground unleashed three more shells into the sage behind them.

ALTHOUGH TRASK HAD ALSO, of course, heard the Abrams approaching, he calculated that he still required at least eighteen minutes to stabilize his assault formation.

Eighteen critical minutes.

He turned to Harris and shoved the radio into the man's hand. "Bring up the fire teams," he said. He lifted an arm above his head to signal the teams on his right flank. He switched on the Starlite scope and slowly scanned the ground to his left. Then, although he once more may have seen someone stalking between the lines of Joshua trees and the obstacle course, a full nine minutes passed before he finally suggested that Harris send out a patrol to investigate.

LYONS AND HIS MEN had already moved into position. The Able Team commando had led thirty-eight members of Black's team along the southern perimeter and on to the left flank of the enemy. He moved them along the drainage ditches and below the lip of a small embankment originally dug to counter flash flooding. Although initially he had been concerned that the footsteps of thirty men would never go unnoticed, he had been amazed at how adept Black's men were at moving silently in the darkness. Even Schwarz and Blancanales, who had served with some of America's best in Vietnam, claimed that they had never seen such noiseless movement.

There were four systems of drainage ditches along the perimeter where Lyons decided to begin his attack. There were also stacked oil drums, scrap timber and sand pits that had been incorporated into the obstacle course. In the face of an advancing Abrams or laser directed machine gun fire, the ground would have proved a death trap. As a launch pad for a fast offensive strike, however, it was almost ideal.

"Once we go," Lyons whispered, "there'll be no turning back."

Blancanales nodded, glanced down the line to Schwarz, Black and three or four others who had slid into the sand pit beside him.

"So what else is new?" he finally breathed.

"I'm just saying that—"

"We know what you're saying," Black interjected. "We know exactly what you're saying."

At which point Lyons nodded, lifted his left arm into the air, and brought it down again in a long, slow arc.

Let's go!

A LOT OF THINGS went through Sergeant Trask's mind as he watched the first three men on his left collapse in a rain of NATO specification rounds. He thought about an ambush he had suffered while on patrol at Khe Sanh: twenty-one dead because someone had neglected to scout the elephant grass. He thought about York Black's men and wondered where they had learned to move so damn silently. He thought about Lyons, Blancanales and Schwarz, and wondered what made men like that tick. But mostly he thought about his own men, and decided that it wasn't their fault. The problem ultimately lay in the fact that the Wolf's Tooth unit had been prepared to meet an untrained civilian force...not a team of crack professionals.

It also crossed Trask's mind that he was probably going to die, and for the life of him he couldn't figure out what he would be dying for.

At least ten men fell before Trask was even able to shout an order to take cover—ten men caught midstride by a withering burst of autofire. Among those first ten were three men that Trask had always counted as friends, and at least four more that he had known since the fall of Saigon. Also among the first casualties was Lieutenant Webber—caught while screaming by six slugs that virtually severed his head from his shoulders.

"Do something!" Harris began screaming. "For God sake's do something!"

There were other screams, most of them unintelligible, as a second and third sustained burst of autofire raked the gravel where Trask and his men lay. Thin clouds of blood and tissue rose from the backs of three men who attempted to shelter themselves behind a clump of creosote. A hand, literally blasted from the wrist of a man, sailed at least six feet in the air before landing on the gravel beside Trask.

"Where are the tanks?" someone screamed. "The tanks!"

But as if in response, Trask heard the wailing hiss of at least four Vipers snaking into targets behind him.

"Medic!" someone screamed as more bullets shredded the huddled bodies.

Trask felt something slam into his left thigh. I've been hit, he thought. *Hit!* But when he slid his hand along his leg, he realized that the bloody wad of flesh was not his own, that a kid named Harcourt had been caught by more than fifteen slugs and pieces of his body were now scattered all over the ground. Judging by the screams from behind a water pipe, Trask was also fairly certain that Harris had been hit....

COLONEL STACK had also heard the screams and for at least three minutes he hadn't been able to move from the window. Here and there among the black humps of Quonset huts and concrete barracks, he had seen flashes of explosions: trailing impressions of hot steel streaking through the darkness, tracks of incendiary bullets and phosphorous. But it was the screams that finally left him paralyzed at the window.

"Colonel? Colonel? Colonel, please, I need a brief!"

Stack turned slowly to face his chief intelligence officer, Arnold Basker. A slender man with a background in languages, Basker had never particularly impressed the colonel. But with dawn still three hours away and enemy fire in the assembly yard, Stack had to admit that the man seemed remarkably cool.

"Just tell me what you want me to do, sir," Basker said as the colonel's blank gaze finally met his own. "Just tell me, sir."

Stack shut his eyes, remaining absolutely motionless for a moment. "Where are they now?" he finally asked. "Where?"

Basker shrugged a tired sigh. "Pretty much all around, sir."

"And the tanks?"

"Four down, two more spewing smoke."

"How about the choppers?"

"Never had a chance to get off the ground."

The lights suddenly dimmed with an explosion not eighty yards away, and there were new cracks of autofire from the assembly ground. Then finally shutting his eyes again, Stack listened for the screams . . . two, three, four trailing screams that cut through the night silence.

"Sir?" Basker whispered. "Sir, if you'd like me to—"

But Stack merely shook his head and pointed to a red telephone on the desk. "Just get me Doyle," he said. "Just get me that bastard Doyle on the line."

23

General Doyle put down the telephone and turned to General Clancy. Clancy, however, was still fixed at the window, staring out to the predawn streets and the gray-and-black van parked in the shadows of a Chinese laundry. He hadn't much cared for the shifting shadows in the apartment window opposite his Georgetown condo. Nor had he liked the fact that a thin man wearing a trench coat was standing beneath the elms in the little park at the end of the lane.

"They're definitely under attack," Doyle said. "Under attack and up against the wall."

Clancy, pulling himself away from the window, reached for his Scotch on the little Queen Anne table. He had also begun smoking again . . . nine years after quitting. "Why?" he breathed. "That's what I want to know. Why?"

Doyle merely shook his head. "What difference does it make? All that matters is that it's happening and we've got to act fast."

"What happened to their tanks?"

"Vipers."

"Their choppers?"

"Hit before they got off the ground."

"Then send them some more. Call for backup from Kirtland."

But again Doyle merely shook his head. "It's too late for that," he said. "It's no longer tactical. It's strategic. If we're going to save this operation, then we're going to have to launch everything now. Tonight."

Clancy drifted over to a laminated liquor cabinet and poured himself another Scotch—his third in the course of an hour. "Don't you think we should at least talk to the others?" he said. "At least put in a call to Jones and Duke?"

"And tell them what? That we're getting the shit kicked out of us?"

Echoes of footsteps on the pavement drew Clancy back to the window. Yet peering down to the lane all he saw were wreaths of dawn mist and more shifting shadows. "All right, then tell me what you're thinking," he said finally. "Just tell me what you're thinking."

"An air strike," Doyle replied. "I'm thinking about an air strike. Something fast and hard to knock those bastards right out of the game."

"And the unit?"

"We'll just have to replace them with one of Duke's teams, or maybe pull in the SEALs."

"What do we tell the civilians?"

"Screw the civilians."

Clancy took another sip of Scotch, then briefly shut his eyes. "All right," he finally nodded, "let's go for it. Go on," he said, his voice suddenly rising in panic. "Make the damn call!"

Doyle reached for the phone, but simply shook his head. "I can't. The phone just went dead."

General Clancy immediately retrieved the .380 Beretta he kept in the middle drawer of the Queen Anne bureau. Yet even before he had time to get a good grip on the weapon, the door burst open.

Lyle Severson entered the room slowly. Behind him were three young men in Levi's and loafers. Although Clancy had never seen the young men before, he concluded that they were operatives from one of the Agency's clandestine branches, probably counterintelligence. Although Severson did not carry a weapon, his long-haired associates were armed with Uzis. Also part of Severson's ragged little retinue was Robert "The Shark" Maloy. The man hardly posed a threat because he was wearing handcuffs.

"I'm sure we'd all be more comfortable if we sat," Severson said. He turned to Clancy and extended his hand to take the Beretta. "Arthur?"

A lean and hungry looking youth called Steggie was ordered to search the bedroom and den, while another young man moved into the kitchen in order to make some coffee. Severson's third associate, a sallow boy who was probably a college student, remained in the corner with a leveled Uzi. Doyle, Clancy and Maloy were told to sit on the couch.

"Think of us as your baby-sitters," Severson said with another smirking smile. "You've been very naughty boys and we can't leave you alone anymore."

"You better believe that I'm going to have your hide for this," Clancy said.

"Shut up, Arthur," Doyle sighed. "Just shut up."

Steggie emerged from the bedroom, with Clancy's telephone book and a handful of correspondence from Admiral Jones. "It looks pretty clean," he said.

"Then check the closets and drawers," Severson replied, "and don't worry about the damage."

"I presume you don't have a warrant," Doyle said.

Severson moved from the window to examine Clancy's collection of etchings. There were two or three dubious Goyas and a plainly bogus Rembrandt. "I don't think a warrant is necessary, since I hardly expect that you gentlemen will ever stand trial."

"Then what the hell do you think you're doing, Severson?" Clancy snapped. "Huh? Just what the hell do you think you're doing?"

"Sparing everyone concerned a great deal of humiliation and embarrassment."

The second youth emerged from the kitchen with a pot of coffee and five cups. "I'm afraid it's instant, sir," he said to Severson, "and I couldn't find the cream."

Severson acknowledged the boy with a nod, and proceeded to pour the coffee. As always his movements were measured and precise. "It's a simple enough situation," he said as he handed Doyle a cup of coffee. "You will remain here with us until the Wolf's Tooth compound has been secured. You will then be delivered to selected members of the Secret Service. The President will order your punishment. Your confederates in this little cabal are also under house arrest."

Doyle accepted the coffee but couldn't seem to bring himself to drink it. "And what happens if the Wolf's Tooth isn't secured?" he asked calmly. "What happens if my boys kick the living shit out of your boys?"

Severson poured a second cup for Clancy, then a third for Maloy. "I hardly think that's likely, judging from the way things are going."

Maloy turned to Doyle and whispered, "He's right, sir. As of an hour ago, things looked bad."

Having finished serving coffee, Severson moved to the window and nodded to someone standing in the street below. Then turning to face the generals again, he continued, "I must admit that your plan was well conceived. In fact, had you only shown a bit more tact, you might have pulled it off." He shifted his gaze from Clancy to Doyle.

"Although you really shouldn't have tried to kill Senator Harwood, and locking up that girl was just plain stupid."

Doyle took a sip of the coffee, but then laid the cup back down again with a disgusted frown. "You know, simply because you don't approve of our methods, Lyle, doesn't necessarily mean that our goals are not justified."

Severson turned with another thin smirk. "Is that so, General?"

Doyle returned the smirk, with a small shrug. "It's axiomatic. For twenty years this nation has been slowly sinking to second-class status. The Japs out-produce us. The Germans outbid us. The Iranians hold us hostage. And if that were not enough, the Russians are setting us up for the biggest fall since Pearl Harbor."

"So you decided to dispense with democracy, was that the plan, General?"

"It was to be a temporary solution. Personally, I have nothing but praise for this nation's Constitution, nothing but undying praise. But the world has changed in the two hundred years since that Constitution was drafted, and some things are simply no longer practical."

"Such as the right to life and liberty?"

Doyle shook his head and uttered a frustrated sigh. "All I can tell you is that drastic situations sometimes require drastic solutions."

"Such as the murder of the President, and God knows how many others?"

Doyle shook his head again, but this time smiled. "As a matter of fact, I have nothing but the greatest respect for the President. In fact, without him this nation's military would never have reached a level of strength wherein such a plan was even conceivable. Ironically, however, the President's case only underscores the necessity of drastic action. For although he basically sees the world as we do and has desperately tried to keep America strong, he is forever hamstrung by a treasonously liberal Congress and Senate. Thus, his failure merely reinforced our convictions . . . reinforced our belief that the time had come for military intervention.''

''And what about the people?'' Severson couldn't help asking. ''What about the two-hundred-and-fifty million American citizens who might disagree with you? What happens to them?''

Doyle shrugged. ''Once they understood the issues at stake, I think they would thank us. I think they would sincereley thank us for having saved this nation from a slow and whimpering death. Not, of course, that it really matters,'' he sighed, ''because in the final analysis the people are sheep—always have been, always will be.''

Several possible responses went through Severson's mind, several hard replies to the general's fascist dogma. But even before he could turn to face the man again, Steggie appeared carrying a cellular phone.

''Excuse me, Mr. Severson,'' the boy whispered, ''but we've just heard from the Wolf's Tooth, and unless these generals order a surrender, their whole unit might end up in body bags.''

Severson nodded, then glanced over his shoulder to Doyle. ''You hear that, General? Unless you tell Stack to surrender, my assault team will have no choice but to chew him and his men into little pieces.''

Doyle looked at Clancy, Clancy at Maloy. Initially, however, none of them said anything.

''Gentlemen,'' Severson implored. ''Gentlemen, there's nothing to be gained at this point by more bloodshed. Call it off. Let me connect you with Stack, and tell him to call it off.''

Once again, however, Doyle simply shook his head, while his eyes remained fixed on the empty space in front him. "My men have their orders," he whispered. "They have their orders."

24

A long stream of blood ran down the steps of the Lincoln Memorial and into the Reflecting Pool. There was also a fair amount of blood on the Capitol building, and still more across Pennsylvania Avenue where three Wolf's Tooth soldiers had been hit while attempting to flee past the fifty-foot game board.

York Black switched off the Starlite scope and scanned the miniaturized mock-up of the Capitol with his naked eye. Laid out in a large square between the assembly quad walls and a solid rank of briefing rooms, the Capitol Hill mock-up rested on a four-foot brick base. There were tables and chairs around the base, and a tarpaulin to protect the model from rain. Although quite crude in many respects, even the little plastic trees looked real in the moonlight...even the eighteen-inch pedestrians, the tiny automobiles and the fiberboard facade of the Senate building. In fact the only thing that seemed unreal was the long stretch of gravel beyond the edge of the game board and the dark forms of sandbags where Colonel Stack had chosen to make his last stand.

"Maybe we should try talking to them?" Blancanales said. "Maybe we should try opening up a little dialogue."

Lyons glanced at Black. "How about it? You think they'd be open to a little reason at this point?"

Black shook his head. "I doubt it," he said. "I seriously doubt it."

"Then what?" Schwarz asked.

Black shrugged and glanced back out across the Capitol mock-up to the plaster replica of the Washington Monument and the fiberboard replica of the Smithsonian Institute. "We're just going to have to start digging them out of there," he said.

They lay in the shadow of the high wall that framed the east boundary of the game court. Across the far gravel lay at least five defensible positions: two bunkers, two more reinforced concrete briefing rooms and another sand-bagged flood control ditch. There was also another Abrams M-1 out there—apparently crippled and probably low on ammunition, but still waiting for action.

A sniper named Caswell returned from a patrol along the adjoining perimeter. After snaking his way through the crouched ranks of men in the assembly quad, he slid into the shadows between Black and Lyons.

"Quiet as a grave out there," he said.

"What about Stack's office?" Black asked.

"That's empty too."

"And the night course?" Lyons asked.

"Just more bodies."

"So then basically they're just holed up out there waiting for us, that it?" Blancanales asked.

Caswell nodded, "Yes, sir, that's it. They're all just out there playing Custer's Last Stand."

Lyons switched on the Starlite scope for yet another scan of the ground beyond the Capitol course.

"Okay then, how about gas?" Schwarz suggested. "How about we pump in a little tear gas?"

Black glanced at Caswell, but the boy just shook his head. "We'd never get close enough, not with that tank and the M-60s."

"Well, there's just got to be a way to end this thing without having to waste any more of them," Lyons said. "There's just got to be."

But after another quick glance at Caswell, Black simply shook his head. "I don't think so, Carl. I think those guys have their orders, that's all there is to it."

"You THINKING what I'm thinking?" Corporal Harris asked.

Trask looked at the wounded man. Harris's face was taut with pain, the eyes laced with red veins. At least an inch of shattered bone showed through the thigh. "I don't know, Harris. What you thinking?"

"I'm thinking this is crazy. I'm thinking that we're all going to end up dying for nothing."

Trask eased his gaze along the sandbag wall to where Colonel Stack sat behind an M-60—eyes fixed on the unreal forms of miniaturized buildings, back rigid, jaw continually working in silence.

"Yeah," Trask finally sighed. "I think it's crazy."

In all there were ninety-two Wolf's Tooth men entrenched behind the concrete and sandbags that formed the edge of the game court. Although possibly not the best sector of the complex for a last stand, it was all that had been finally available. Trask secretly suspected that Stack liked the idea of fighting and dying around the fifty square foot mock-up of his nation's capital. He liked the idea of fighting and dying over bits of plastic, fiberboard and chicken wire.

A bulky sergeant named Murphy slid down behind the bunker beside Trask. In addition to his assault rifle, the man had packed at least ten grenades in a canvas satchel that he wore across his shoulder.

"Colonel wants you two to prepare to move out," Murphy said.

Trask looked at the sergeant, then again at Harris's shattered leg. "You got to be kidding."

Murphy shook his head. "No, I ain't kidding. In exactly seven minutes we're going to be bringing an Abrams through here...starting that sucker up and bringing it right through this here position. So if you boys don't want to be turned into hamburger, I suggest that you start moving."

Harris and Trask exchanged another glance: Harris actually smiling through the pain and haze of morphine, while Trask simply shook his head.

But as the sergeant slid back into the shadows, Trask suddenly couldn't keep himself from whispering it again, "Yeah, this is definitely crazy."

ALTHOUGH THE M-1 ABRAMS had suffered two hits from Vipers, knocking out its long-range sighting system and damaging a turbine, it was still maneuverable. It still packed fifteen 120 mm shells, and nearly two hundred rounds on the machine gun belts.

"Looks like they're going to use it to try and punch themselves a hole," Schwarz said. "Bring her right up on that little White House lawn, and kick us in the teeth."

Having slid out across the pavement to the low concrete wall that formed the edge of the Capitol Hill mock-up, he and Lyons finally had a clear view past the mock-up to the entrenchments some two hundred yards across the gravel. At one point, scanning the ground with a hand-held night-vision system, Schwarz had even caught a glimpse of Stack: still fixed behind the M-60, and still obviously determined. Then upon hearing the echo of rumbling treads on the gravel, the Able Team commando had turned his gaze to the tank.

"Sounds like a Chevy with a broken rod," Lyons whispered as the echo of the tank grew louder.

"Don't kid yourself," Schwarz replied. "As long as that thing can move and shoot, we got problems."

"So what do you think we should do about it?"

Schwarz glanced over his shoulder at the dim outline of Black and Blancanales still crouched in the shadow of the assembly wall. "I think we'd better get some of those Vipers up here . . . and fast."

Lyons withdrew a mini Mag-Lite and rapidly switched it on and off three times. But even if Black had been watching, he couldn't possibly have seen the tiny blinking light what with the flash of the Abrams's main gun.

The explosion seemed to suck the oxygen out of the air, leaving Lyons breathing only hot gas. It also did strange things to his spine, and left a taste of old pennies in his mouth. He tried to scream, but words only came out in a whisper. Then trying to rise to his feet, he felt as if an elephant was kneeling on his chest.

"Got to get out of here," he finally managed to whisper. "Got to get the hell out of here."

He was also conscious of blood on his face, and he couldn't seem to hear anything except ringing bells.

"Where's the Viper teams?" Schwarz whispered, ignoring Lyons. "Where the hell are those damn Viper teams?"

There were four long bursts from an M-60, while another Abrams shell took out twelve feet of the assembly quad wall. There were also cries of at least three soldiers who must have been caught by fragments of brick and gravel. Schwarz pressed himself closer to the wall, withdrew a grenade, but then simply swore under his breath.

"Holy shit!" he finally yelled as the hulking outline of the Abrams M-1 emerged above the sandbags.

The tank was advancing at a slow pace, no more than three or four miles per hour. Behind it were at least forty men, armed with assault rifles, grenade launchers and M-16s. Although Schwarz may have also caught another glimpse of Stack, he couldn't be certain of anything once that big gun opened up again...leaving him literally kissing the ground in a shower of hot rocks and plaster.

ALTHOUGH ALSO PRESSED to the ground and shuddering with shock waves, Black and Blancanales were ready. When one of the big shells tore out nine feet of brick above their heads, Black merely shook his head and grinned.

"I hate it when your fillings start shaking loose," he laughed. "I just hate it when that happens."

Another shell from the turret gun slammed into the gravel behind them, and there were reverberations of machine guns tearing out chunks of brick. But having finally managed to slide back into the drainage ditch, Black called back for his Vipers.

Weighing about nine pounds and capable of penetrating sixteen inches of armor, the Viper antitank missile had originally been developed when earlier tube launched weapons had proved themselves ineffective against the new generation of Warsaw Pact vehicles. Initial test results of the Viper still raised criticisms regarding effectiveness, but nothing that Black or Blancanales were concerned about...particularly considering the range.

There was a long and narrow stretch of gravel between the assembly wall and the briefing huts. As the Abrams drew closer to the Capitol mock-up, Blancanales slid into the doorway of the last briefing hut and lifted the plastic sight. Beside him was a wiry Cajun boy named Balzar, who kept whispering, "Easy, mister. Easy, mister." Then as the Abrams drew even closer, less than sixty feet from the line of fire, he said, "Kick it now, man! Now!"

Blancanales fired for the turret mount. He fired with both eyes open, but his concentration was fixed only on the target. He fired with the full knowledge that his target was an American vehicle, manned by an American team. He fired with a taste of vomit in his mouth and a deeper disgust in the pit of his stomach.

There was a muffled thump, like a bundle of wet newspapers falling on a steel drum, then an echoing crack of ripping steel and a long tongue of white flame. Fragments of shrapnel, spraying into the ranks behind, instantly dropped at least three men. Four or five more began screaming with leg wounds and shoulder wounds. There may have also been screams from inside the tank, hollow and desperate, but they were soon cut off by a second Viper, slamming under the gun mount.

The Abrams lurched again as Black's missile struck from the opposite side, almost bucking for an instant in a blue-green flash of light. Simultaneously there were more screams from the men behind the tank as Black's forward team opened up with their MP-5s, spraying more lead from the drainage ditch and briefing huts. At least six Wolf's Tooth soldiers instantly crumpled, writhing under the impact of the NATO specification rounds, while another ten or twenty simply broke rank and ran. A tall sniper named Hutchenson, catching two slugs in the thigh, sank to his knees with a grenade. But before he could pull the pin, another seven slugs turned his face and shoulders to a bloody pulp.

"Move!" Black was shouting. "Move! Move! Move!"

Blancanales tossed the firing tube away and reached for his assault rifle. Yet before he could even drop the safety, he saw at least three men shivering with the impact of spray from Schwarz's weapon. Moments later Lyons was also on his feet, pouring fire over the Washington Monument and into a cluster of Wolf's Tooth riflemen.

Although the Abrams's guns were silent, two of Black's men had finally climbed onto the stationary hulk. They pried open a damaged hatch, hesitated a moment, then dropped in two grenades. There was an audible scream and the echo of ripping steel and pounding shrapnel from within the belly of the tank.

"Move!" Black shouted again. "Move it *now*!"

Between twenty and thirty of Black's men immediately responded to the order, slipping out of the drainage ditch and pressing the attack. When five Wolf's Tooth soldiers attempted to delay them, dropping to their knees and opening up with their M-16s, Black's men simply tossed more grenades.

There were two distinct screams in response to the grenades. The first was frantic, almost a plea. The second was simply insane. Then although there was some return fire from the bunkers, most of the Wolf's Tooth survivors seemed concerned with just keeping themselves alive. Even Stack, Blancanales noticed, had apparently abandoned his weapon and slipped behind the sandbags.

Still more screams broke as Black's team began squeezing off shells from their grenade launchers. But before Black could bring up his main team and his three M-60s, Lyons called out for a cease-fire . . . firing half a magazine into the air, and shouting to Black that it had gone far enough . . . *far enough*.

Having drawn within fifty yards of the sandbags, Lyons slid into an electrical shed and laid his assault rifle down. Watching from the deeper shadows were two wounded Wolf's Tooth soldiers: a slim kid named Wiley who had taken a slug in the hip, and a beefy sergeant named Eagleton who was very close to death with a bullet in the throat. Although both men were apparently trying to remain silent, their ragged breath and occasional moans were still audible. Beyond the shed lay at least another dozen bodies on the gravel, while three or four more may have been whimpering from the first row of sandbags. Otherwise, the compound was quiet.

Black appeared, leading eight or ten men with M-203 grenade launchers attached to M-16A1 automatic rifles, with a cyclical rate of 650-850 rounds per minute. One of the men, a dark and unusually silent killer named Laplin, also carried a new M-224 mortar. Beyond them were Schwarz and Blancanales. There was simply no telling, however, where Black had stationed the others.

"We can pop 'em from right here," Black said softly. "I got another thirty guys circling around the back to cut them off from the fence, so all you got to do is give the word and we can pop 'em right where it counts."

Lyons slid down to one knee, and peered out through the blasted door of the hut for a better look at the nearly silent wall of sandbags and the apparently empty concrete briefing rooms. What had initially seemed to be someone waving, however, was finally just another piece of loose debris snapping in the wind.

"Why don't you just give me the options in plain and simple terms?" Lyons said at last.

Black inched up next to the big man and also ran his gaze along the sandbags. "Like I said," he whispered, "I'll have them cut off in about seven minutes. Then we can either finish them off with grenades, or maybe even hit them with a few more Vipers and that mortar."

"What about the guys in those concrete briefing rooms?"

Black shrugged. "What about them? You squeeze off a couple of Vipers, and that'll be the end of that...believe me, Carl."

But after yet another long scan of the ground ahead—the littered bodies, the gently shifting shadows that may have been still more wounded men—Lyons simply shook his head. He took a long, hard breath, then just shook his head and whispered, "No. No, I don't think so."

Black looked at him. "What do you mean?"

"I mean that we can't just go on killing those guys, not without giving them a chance to surrender."

"Fine. I'll find you a bullhorn, and we'll give them a chance to surrender."

"No," Lyons sighed. "Not with the bullhorn. I want to meet them face-to-face...right out there in the open, face-to-face."

"Suit yourself," Black shrugged. "But if they blow your head off, it's not my fault."

LYONS MOVED OUT SLOWLY, hesitating briefly with a last thin smile at Black and Blancanales, then continuing into the shadowy darkness between the row of electrical huts and the scorched walls of a laundry room. He kept his empty left hand clearly visible, and the white rag in his right hand above his head. He kept his eyes fixed on the sandbags ahead, and his ears attuned to the slightest sounds. At five or ten yards he heard what may have been a cocking bolt. Otherwise, however, it was still very quiet.

"Stack!" he shouted. Then again after taking yet another five or six steps closer to the wall of sandbags. "Stack, it's Lyons. Can you hear me?"

More silence, and then what may have been another cocking weapon.

"Staaaaaaaaaak!"

"What do you want?" Stack shouted from behind a far mound of sandbags.

"Talk?"

"About what?"

"About saving your life and the lives of your men."

There were six or seven more seconds of silence before Stack finally rose to his feet—a rigid and still entirely determined figure not forty yards away. Behind him were the heads and shoulders of at least twenty other Wolf's Tooth soldiers, who may have been starting to wonder if Lyons had a point. The others, however, remained crouched behind the sandbags.

Lyons briefly shifted his gaze to the far end of the sandbag wall, caught a glimpse of other cautious silhouettes rising into view, then took another four or five steps closer.

"It's over," he shouted. "You understand what I'm saying, Stack? It's over. We've got teams closing in from behind you. We have half a dozen grenade launchers ready to fire. We have mortar fixing your position as I talk. And if you haven't guessed already, your generals are under arrest. So why don't you just give it up? How about it, Colonel? Maybe it's time to just give it up?"

Stack seemed to hesitate before replying, then finally just shrugged. "I've got my orders, Lyons. I've got my orders, and that's all there is to it."

"Your orders are illegal, Colonel. Your orders are contradictory to every law of this land. Your orders were intended to destroy this government and if you die following those orders no one will care...least of all the generals who issued them."

Again Stack seemed to hesitate, possibly weighing Lyons's words, possibly just using this opportunity to scan the ground and target his enemy.

"All right," Stack finally sighed. "Then tell me what you have in mind."

Lyons glanced to the left where three or four of Stack's men had risen above the sandbags to watch. Although Sergeant Trask may have been one of them, he couldn't be sure.

"You tell your men to lay down their weapons, and I'll guarantee you safe passage out of here," Lyons shouted. "I will personally guarantee you safe passage out."

"So we can face a Senate hearing? So we can spend the next twenty years in the federal pen? No thanks, Lyons. No thanks."

"Look, it doesn't have to go down that way and you know it, Colonel," Lyons countered. Then glancing along the sandbags again into the expectant faces of Stack's men, "You don't have the right to commit your men to death. You just don't have that right."

"You wanna bet?" Stack smiled. Then he slowly raised his pistol, extending it with a stiff arm toward Lyons's face, "You wanna bet?"

Lyons shouted the colonel's name before he dropped, shouted as much out of rage as anything else. Then catching another glimpse of the colonel's silhouette behind the muzzle of the Browning, he shouted out the name again "*Staaack!*"

But when the shots finally broke, they weren't from Stack's Browning.

Sergeant Trask fired three rounds into the colonel's back, three quick rounds from his MP-5. Before the colonel actually fell, however, someone else—Corporal Harris—also squeezed off a couple of shots. In response the colonel seemed to hesitate again, back arched with the impact, arms flung out from his body...then finally glancing back over his shoulder in surprise, he collapsed across the sandbags.

"This is crazy," Trask whispered. "This is completely crazy."

IT WAS DAWN before some semblance of order had been restored to the Wolf's Tooth compound. Although the wind had finally subsided, the cold remained—a deep chill that seemed to rise up from the desert canyons and vaguely smelled of creosote. Although Black's team worked quickly and efficiently with the wounded, at least four more finally bled to death before they could be reached: two in the drainage ditches, one amid a litter of bricks and scrap metal, and still another beside the mock-up of the Capitol.

"I've called in choppers from over the hill," Black said. "I don't know what you're going to tell him, but at least we'll be able to get the wounded out of here."

Lyons accepted a flask of brandy from Black, took a swig and then sank to the sandbags. Among the bodies that still lay uncollected along the rubble-strewn stretch of gravel were two Wolf's Tooth soldiers who had fallen on that mock-up of the capital: a slender corporal who appeared to be reaching for the Lincoln Memorial, and a sniper named Hawkins who had collapsed in the plastic shrubbery.

"So how about it?" Black said after another two or three minutes of silence.

"How about what?" Lyons asked.

"What are we supposed to tell people about what happened here?"

Lyons shook his head, with a long and hard breath. "I don't know. I just don't know."

25

Senator Harwood gazed up into the stony eyes of Abraham Lincoln, and sank back down to the chilled marble. "What would you have done, Mr. President?" he whispered. "What would you have done?"

Although still very cold with a wind off the river and ice along the Reflecting Pool there seemed to be children everywhere. They had poured out of buses from as far away as Colorado and Kansas to visit their nation's capital. There were also a fair number of older tourists: senior citizen groups from Miami and Tampa, veterans groups from New York and Boston, historical societies from all points west. For the moment, however, Harwood saw only Lincoln's eyes, saw them as he had never seen them before.

"I think he would have done exactly what we're going to do," Lyle Severson said after a long silence. "I think he would have swept it all under the rug and let the wounds heal."

Harwood shifted his gaze from the statue of Lincoln to the glistening dome of the Capitol. "You think so?" he asked bitterly. "You really think so? Well, I don't. I don't think that's what Lincoln would have done at all."

Severson turned his collar up against the wind, and jammed his hands in his pockets. Although he was due to breakfast at the White House in less than twenty minutes, he felt that he owed it to Harwood to at least answer the man's questions . . . to stand and face the senator's questions.

"Look at it this way," Severson said suddenly. "You drag those generals before a Senate committee, then make them stand trial for treason, and this nation will never recover its trust in our military . . . never."

"Yeah?" Well, maybe that's not such a bad thing," Harwood countered. "Maybe we shouldn't trust the military. Maybe we should subject them to the closest damn scrutiny possible, because maybe that's the only way to keep those bastards from turning this country into a police state!"

Severson laid a hand on Harwood's shoulder and began to lead him down the steps. Years ago, shortly after the death of Harwood's wife, they had walked more than a mile this way: eyes locked on the gray pavement, Severson's arm around Harwood's narrow shoulder. And the tone of Severson's voice had been the same—soft and soothing.

"You know, sometimes you just have to tell yourself that the nightmare is over, old horse," Severson said. "Sometimes you just have to tell yourself that it was all a bad dream, and now it's over."

They paused by the Reflecting Pool to watch another line of children marching under the leafless trees. Pigeons, attracted by discarded candy wrappers and peanut shells, were patrolling the sidewalks.

"So how does it end?" Harwood said at last. "Just tell me how it ends, Lyle."

"I rather think you're not going to approve," Severson replied.

"Just tell me."

"Very well," Severson sighed. "There's not going to be an investigation, not a public one at any rate."

"Then what will there be?"

"The generals are simply going to tender their resignations, the President is going to accept those resignations and that will be the end of that."

"Except, of course, that Doyle and the others will probably end up taking advisory positions at TRW or Hughes Aircraft at seventy-five grand a year plus stock options and whatever else they can skim off the top."

"I didn't say it was to be fair, John. I simply said that it was an ending."

"And what happens to the Wolf's Tooth? What happens to all those poor bastards that survived the assault?"

"Some will be discharged, some will be transferred, some will just slip back into the woodwork."

"Until some other lunatic general comes along with a plan to conquer the world? Is that it, Lyle? Is that the point of this little settlement?"

They paused again where the broad lawns fell away to sculpted hedgerows. Although the children were no longer in sight the voice of their teacher was still audible: a vaguely shrill woman, explaining that Abraham Lincoln not only freed the slaves, but also kept the nation from being torn asunder.

"What happens if somebody talks?" Harwood said suddenly. "What happens if someone from *Frontline* gets wind of the story, and contacts one of those Able Team fellows? Hmm? What happens then?"

Severson shook his head. "I think it's rather unlikely. Besides, Lyons and his people are professional soldiers, not publicity hounds. They're part of a covert operation—they will not go public with *any* information."

"All right, but what happens if one of the Wolf's Tooth survivors suddenly decides to talk? What are you going to do about that?"

Again, however, Severson simply shook his head. "At this point, I really don't think it's a realistic concern. After all, those men are getting off easy and they know it. I hardly think that they'll want to publicize their role as traitors. Do you?"

A second teacher, a thin young woman in a yellow raincoat, had begun to discuss Thomas Jefferson's role in the framing of the Bill of Rights. There were also echoes of circling choppers, probably from one of the local news stations.

"But that still leaves the girl," Harwood said.

Severson cocked his head to the side. "The girl?"

"Molly Meekin. What happens if she decides that the nation ultimately has a right to know? What happens if she decides to write a book about it all? Hmm? What the hell are you going to do about that one, Lyle?"

Severson shrugged with a small sigh. "Then I suppose that I'll simply have to send someone to talk to her," he replied. "Someone persuasive."

"Well, I don't like it one bit," Harwood breathed, "not one little bit."

Again, however, Severson merely shrugged. "You're not supposed to like it, John. You're simply supposed to be glad that this nation is still relatively democratic, and leave it at that."

26

Carl Lyons took another sip of beer, and stared into the vaguely sad eyes of Thomas Jefferson. Although the sun had set more than an hour ago, leaving the bedroom of Severson's country safehouse bathed in shadows, he hadn't bothered to switch on the lamp. He had also switched off the television midway through the President's speech and had tossed the newspaper into the fire. There were now no sounds at all, except for the call of night birds and the gentle whisper of Molly Meekin's breath.

She lay on the low divan by the window—a sleepy storm of hair across her cheek, the senator's Brooks Brothers shirt barely covering her slender thighs. Although he could not see her eyes he knew that she was watching him again—lips parted in a half smile, her thoughts a thousand miles away.

"What do you think he would have had to say about all this?" she suddenly asked.

Lyons crushed the can and tossed it into the fireplace. "Who?"

She pointed to the portrait above the hearth. "Thomas Jefferson. How do you think he would have felt about what happened at the Wolf's Tooth?"

Lyons met that vaguely tragic gaze again, then simply shrugged. "I don't know," he sighed. "Maybe he would have just been happy that it's over."

Molly seemed to consider Lyons's words for a moment, but finally shook her head. "Well, I don't think so. I think he would have wanted to ensure that it never happened again. I think he would have wanted to make sure that nothing like it ever happens again."

Lyons turned in his chair to face her. "What are you talking about, Molly?"

She rose to her knees, the senator's shirt slipping past her left shoulder, moonlight playing on her freckles, her right breast nearly exposed.

"I'm talking about writing it all down," she said. "I'm talking about writing it all down and then publishing it— maybe as my political science thesis. I mean, it's got to be worth at least a master's degree."

Lyons stretched out a hand to stroke her cheek. "You know, I really don't think that would be such a good idea. You understand what I'm saying? I just don't think that would be such a good idea."

"Why not?"

"Because there are a lot of people out there who have a vested interest in sweeping this thing under the rug . . . very powerful people, people who would go to all kinds of lengths to make sure that you don't tell your story."

Molly shrugged so that the shirt slipped even lower across her shoulder. "Oh, I don't think they'll bother me," she said. "I don't think they'll bother me one little bit."

"Why do you say that?"

She took his hand from her cheek, and pressed it to her breast. "Because I got you," she smiled.

More than action adventure...
books written by the men who were there

VIETNAM: GROUND ZERO.™

ERIC HELM

Told through the eyes of an American Special Forces squad, an
elite jungle fighting group of strike-and-hide specialists fight a
dirty war half a world away from home.

These books cut close to the bone, telling it the way it
really was.

"Vietnam at Ground Zero is where this book is
written. The author has been there, and he knows.
I salute him and I recommend this book to my
friends."
—Don Pendleton
creator of *The Executioner*

"Helm writes in an evocative style that gives us Nam as
it most likely was, without prettying up or undue
bitterness."
—*Cedar Rapids Gazette*

"Eric Helm's Vietnam series embodies a literary
standard of excellence. These books linger in the
mind long after their reading."
—*Midwest Book Review*

Available wherever paperbacks are sold.

VIE 1

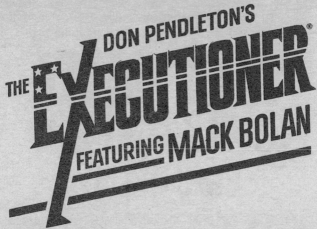

DON PENDLETON'S THE EXECUTIONER®
FEATURING MACK BOLAN

Baptized in the fire and blood of Vietnam, Mack Bolan has become America's supreme hero. Fiercely patriotic and compassionate, he's a man with a high moral code whose sense of right and wrong sometimes violates society's rules. In adventures filled with heart-stopping action, Bolan has thrilled readers around the world. Experience the high-voltage charge as Bolan rallies to the call of his own conscience in daring exploits that place him in peril with virtually every heartbeat.

"Anyone who stands against the civilized forces of truth and justice will sooner or later have to face the piercing blue eyes and cold Beretta steel of Mack Bolan...civilization's avenging angel."
—*San Francisco Examiner*

GOLD EAGLE

Available wherever paperbacks are sold.

MB-2RR